Mya placed her hand over Giles's.
"Are you living out your dream?"

A mysterious smile tilted the corners of his mouth. "I am. Before I met you, my sole focus was on work, and the harder I worked, the more I was able to convince myself that I didn't need or want anyone to share my life." He pressed his forehead to hers. "Meeting you has proven me wrong. Not only do I want you, but I need you."

Mya closed her eyes, too stunned to cry. Men had told her they needed her, but those were glibly spoken words they believed she wanted to hear. She felt his hand shake slightly under hers and in that instant she was aware of the power she wielded over Giles. That he'd shown her vulnerability for the first time.

"I need you, too." Her voice was barely a whisper.

* * *

AMERICAN HEROES:
They're coming home—and finding love!

Dear Reader,

I have lost count of the number of requests for another Wainwright title since I introduced Jordan in *Because of You* and his cousin Brandt in *Here I Am*. It has been a long time coming, and now it is Giles Wainwright's turn to take center stage in my second book set in Wickham Falls: *Claiming the Captain's Baby*.

After a stint in the Marine Corps, Giles joins his family's New York City real-estate empire to start up their international division. The confirmed bachelor enjoys his unencumbered lifestyle jetting between the United States and the Caribbean to buy and sell private islands. Giles never could have imagined a request for him to attend the reading of a will in Wickham Falls, West Virginia, would reveal that his brief affair had resulted in him fathering a child.

Within seconds of Giles Wainwright walking into the lawyer's office, Mya Lawson forces herself not to panic. It takes a single glance for her to know that the man is Lily's father. Her terminally ill sister, who refused to name her baby's father, had arranged for Mya to adopt her daughter. Mya isn't prepared for Giles, who is not above using his family's name and wealth to claim his daughter, yet she has no intention of going against her late-sister's wish for Lily to grow up in Wickham Falls. Mya has sacrificed her teaching career to become a full-time mother, while Giles has to decide whether he is willing to give up the fast-paced, glamorous and edgy chic of Manhattan to claim his daughter—and her new mother.

Happy reading!

Rochelle Alers

Claiming the Captain's Baby

—

Rochelle Alers

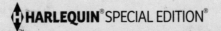

HARLEQUIN® SPECIAL EDITION®

Recycling programs
for this product may
not exist in your area.

ISBN-13: 978-1-335-46551-1

Claiming the Captain's Baby

Copyright © 2017 by Rochelle Alers

Printed in U.S.A.

Since 1988, national bestselling author **Rochelle Alers** has written more than eighty books and short stories. She has earned numerous honors, including the Zora Neale Hurston Literary Award, the Vivian Stephens Award for Excellence in Romance Writing and a Career Achievement Award from *RT Book Reviews*. She is a member of Zeta Phi Beta Sorority, Inc., Iota Theta Zeta Chapter. A full-time writer, she lives in a charming hamlet on Long Island. Rochelle can be contacted through her website, www.rochellealers.org.

Chapter One

Mya Lawson sat staring out the window in her home office as she waited for the pages she had revised to fill the printer's tray. She was still amazed that she had come up with yet another plot for her fictional New England series. What had begun as a hobby for Mya was now a vocation since she gave up her position as college professor to become a stay-at-home mother.

The sound of the printer spitting out paper competed with the incessant tapping of rain against the windows. It had begun raining earlier that morning and had continued nonstop throughout the midafternoon. Mya knew it was an indoor play day for Lily once she woke from her nap. An unconscious smile parted her lips when her gaze lingered on the oak tree shading the backyard. Mya lost count of the number of times she and her sister hid behind the massive trunk or climbed

the thick branches once they were older while playing
hide-and-seek with their mother. Although aware of
their hiding places, Veronica Lawson elected to play
along much to the delight of her rambunctious daughters. But as they grew older the game stopped because
Veronica claimed she did not have the energy to chase
after them.

An expression of melancholy sweeping over Mya's
features replaced her smile. She and seven-month-
old Lily were the last of the Wickham Falls Lawsons.
What she found ironic was that neither she nor Lily
shared DNA with their namesake ancestors. Graham
and Veronica Lawson, after more than twenty years of
a childless marriage, had decided to adopt. They adopted Mya, and then two years later Samantha joined
the family.

Mya exhaled an audible sigh. Her parents were gone,
Samantha was gone, and now there was only she and
her niece.

Her sister wanted Mya to raise Lily in Wickham
Falls—a small town with a population of little more
than four thousand residents—even though Samantha
had complained about growing up in a small town and
couldn't wait to grow up and leave to see the world.
She got her wish once she began her career as a flight
attendant and got to visit many of the cities and countries she had fantasized about.

Sammie, as Mya always called her, had died a month
ago and Mya was still attempting to adjust to the loss
and her life without her sister. Sammie had returned
to Wickham Falls for a rare visit with the news that
she was six weeks pregnant. She told Mya of her affair
with a New York City businessman, and despite using

protection, she'd gotten pregnant. Her sister refused to disclose the name of her lover or tell him about the baby because he had been adamant when he told her he wasn't ready for marriage or fatherhood.

The sudden ring of the telephone shattered her reverie. Unconsciously her brow furrowed when she recognized the name of the law firm that had handled Sammie's will. She picked up the receiver before the second ring.

"Hello."

"Ms. Mya Lawson?"

Mya nodded before she realized the person on the other end of the line could not see her. "Yes. This is she."

"Ms. Lawson, I'm Nicole Campos, Mr. McAvoy's assistant. He'd like you to keep your calendar open for next Thursday because he needs you to come into the office to discuss your daughter's future."

Her frown deepened. "Ms. Campos, can you give me an idea of what he wants to talk about?"

"I'm sorry, but I cannot reveal that information over the telephone."

Twin emotions of annoyance and panic gripped her. She did not want to relive the anxiety she had experienced before the court finalized her adopting her niece. "What time on Thursday?"

"Eleven o'clock. I'll call you the day before as a reminder and follow-up with an email."

Mya exhaled an inaudible sigh. "Thank you."

She hadn't realized her hand was shaking when she replaced the receiver in the console. Leaning back in the desk chair, she combed her fingers through a wealth of brown curly hair with natural gold highlights, holding it off her forehead.

There never had been a question that she would lose Lily to the foster care system because her sister had drawn up a will that included a clause naming Mya as legal guardian for her unborn baby.

A week after Sammie gave birth to a beautiful dark-haired infant, she handed Lily to Mya with the pronouncement that she wanted Mya to raise her daughter as her own. At first she thought Sammie was experiencing postpartum depression, but nothing could have prepared her for the reality that her younger sister was terminally ill.

Sammie had been diagnosed with an aggressive form of breast cancer. Mya put up a brave front for her sister because she needed to be strong for her, but whenever she was alone she could not stop crying. The young, beautiful, vivacious thirty-two-year-old woman who was in love with life was dying and there was nothing she could do to help her.

Gurgling sounds came from the baby monitor on a side table. Mya glanced at the screen where she could observe her daughter. It was after three and Lily was awake.

Pushing back her chair, she rose and walked out of the office and down the hall to the nursery. Lily was standing up in her crib. She'd sat up at five months, began crawling at six and now at seven was able to pull up and stand, but only holding onto something. It was as if her precocious daughter was in a hurry to walk before her first birthday.

Months before Lily's birth, Mya and Sammie spent hours selecting furniture and decorating the room that would become the nursey. The colors of sage green and pale pink were repeated in blankets, quilts and in the colorful border along the antique-white walls.

"Hey, doll baby. Did you have a good nap?"

A squeal of delight filled the space when the baby raised her chubby arms to be picked up. The instant she let go of the railing, Lily landed hard on her bottom but didn't cry. Mya reached over the rail of the crib and scooped her up while scrunching up her nose. She dropped a kiss on damp, inky-black curls. "Somebody needs changing."

Lily pushed out her lips in an attempt to mirror Mya's expression. Mya smiled at the beautiful girl with long dark lashes framing a pair of large sky blue eyes. Lily looked nothing like Sammie, so it was obvious she had inherited her father's hair and eye color.

She placed her on the changing table and took off the damp onesie and then the disposable diaper. At thirty-four, Mya had not planned on becoming a mother, yet learned quickly. She'd read countless books on feedings, teething, potty training and the average milestones for crawling, walking and talking. She had childproofed the house—all the outlets were covered, there were safety locks on the kitchen cabinets and drawers, wires secured off the floor, and all furniture with sharp edges were placed out of the way.

She gathered Lily in her arms and pressed a kiss to her forehead. "You're getting heavy."

Lily grabbed several strands of Mya's hair as she carried her down the staircase to the kitchen. "If you keep pulling my hair, I'll be forced to get extensions." She had made it a habit to either style her hair in a single braid or ponytail because her daughter appeared transfixed by the profusion of curls resembling a lion's mane.

She entered the kitchen and placed Lily in her high chair. Opening the refrigerator, she took out a bottle of milk and filled a sippy cup. Lily screamed in delight when handed the cup.

Mya felt a warm glow flow through her as she watched Lily drink. Her daughter's life would mirror her biological mother's and her aunt's. She would grow up not knowing her birth mother, but Mya had started a journal chronicling the baby's milestones, photographs of Sammie and a collection of postcards from the different cities and countries her sister had visited. Once Lily was old enough to understand that her aunt wasn't her biological mother, Mya would reveal the circumstances of her birth.

"Giles, Brandt is on line two."

The voice of Giles Wainwright's administrative assistant coming through the intercom garnered his attention. He had spent the past twenty minutes going over the architect's rendering and the floor plan of six three-bedroom, two-bath homes on an island in the Bahamas he had recently purchased for the international division of Wainwright Developers Group.

He tapped a button on the intercom. "Thank you, Jocelyn." He activated the speaker feature as he leaned back in the executive chair and rested his feet on the corner of the antique desk. "What's up, cousin?"

"I'm calling to let you know Ciara and I have finally set a date for our wedding."

Brandt "The Viking" Wainwright's professional football career was cut short when he broke both legs in an automobile accident. Sidelined for the season and confined to his penthouse suite, Brandt had had a revolving door of private duty nurses before no-nonsense Ciara Dennison refused to let him bully her. In the end, Brandt realized he had met his match *and* his soul mate.

"Finally," Giles teased. "When is it?"

"We've decided on February 21 at the family resort in the Bahamas. It's after the Super Bowl, and that week the schools are out for winter break. And if adults want to bring their kids, then the more the merrier."

Giles smiled. "I'm certain you won't find an argument from the kids who'd rather hang out on a tropical beach than ski upstate."

Brandt's deep chuckle came through the speaker. "You're probably right about that. Ciara's mailing out the Save the Week notice to everyone. If the family is amenable to spending the week in the tropics, then I'll make arrangements to reserve several villas to accommodate everyone."

Giles listened as Brandt talked about their relatives choosing either to fly down on the corporate jet that seated eighteen, or sail down on the *Mary Catherine*, the Wainwright family yacht. Giles preferred sailing as his mode of transportation, because two to three times a month he flew down to the Bahamas to meet with the broker overseeing the sale of two dozen private islands now owned by Wainwright Developers Group International, or WDG, Inc.

The conversation segued to the news that there would be another addition to the Wainwright clan when Jordan and his wife, Aziza, welcomed their first child in the coming weeks.

Giles lowered his feet and sat straight when Jocelyn Lewis knocked softly on the door and stuck her head through the opening. She held an envelope in one hand.

Giles beckoned her in. "Hold on, Brandt, I need to get something from my assistant."

"I know you're busy, Giles, so I'll talk to you later," Brandt said.

"Give Ciara my love."

"I'll tell her."

Giles ended the call, stood up and took the letter from Jocelyn's outstretched hand. He thought of the woman as a priceless diamond after he had gone through a number of assistants in the four years since he'd started up the overseas division. Within minutes of Giles interviewing her, he had known Jocelyn was the one. At forty-six, she had left her position as director of a childcare center because she wanted to experience the corporate world. What prompted Giles to hire her on the spot was her admission that she'd taken several courses to become proficient in different computer programs.

He met the eyes of the woman who only recently had begun wearing makeup after terminating her membership with a church that frowned on women wearing pants and makeup. The subtle shade of her lipstick complemented the yellow undertones in her flawless mahogany complexion. "Who delivered this?" he asked, when he noticed that the stamp and the postmark were missing. Personal and Confidential was stamped below the addressee, while the return address indicated a Wickham Falls, West Virginia, law firm.

Jocelyn's eyebrows lifted slightly behind a pair of

horn-rimmed glasses. "George brought it up. He said it came with this morning's FedEx delivery."

Giles nodded. "Thank you." All mail for the company was left at the front desk. The receptionist signed for documents requiring a signature, and then she alerted the mail room where George logged in and distributed letters and packages to their respective departments.

Jocelyn hesitated and met her boss's eyes. "I just want to remind you that I'll be in late tomorrow morning. I have to renew my driver's license."

He nodded. Jocelyn had saved his department thousands when she redesigned the website from ordinary to extraordinary with photos of Bahamian-Caribbean style homes on private islands with breathtaking views of the Atlantic Ocean and others with incredibly pristine Caribbean beaches.

Waiting until she walked out of the office and closed the door behind her, Giles sat down and slid a letter opener under the flap of the envelope. A slight frown settled into his features when he read and reread the single page of type. He was being summoned to the reading of a will. The letter did not indicate to whom the will belonged, but requested he call to confirm his attendance.

Picking up the telephone receiver, he tapped the area code and then the numbers. "This is Giles Wainwright," he said, introducing himself when the receptionist identified the name of the law firm. "I have a letter from your firm requesting my presence at the reading of a will this coming Thursday."

There came a pause. "Please hold on, Mr. Wainwright, while I connect you to Mr. McAvoy's office."

Giles drummed his fingers on the top of the mahogany desk with a parquetry inlay.

"Mr. Wainwright, I'm Nicole Campos, Mr. McAvoy's assistant. Are you calling to confirm your attendance?"

"I can't confirm until I know who named me in their will."

"I'm sorry, Mr. Wainwright, but I cannot disclose that at this time."

He went completely still. "You expect me to fly from New York to West Virginia on a whim?"

"It's not a whim, Mr. Wainwright. Someone from your past indicated your name in a codicil to their will. If you choose not to come, then we'll consider the matter settled."

Giles searched his memory for someone he'd met who had come from West Virginia. The only person that came to mind was a soldier under his command when they were deployed to Afghanistan.

Corporal John Foley had lost an eye when the Humvee in which he was riding was hit by shrapnel from a rocket-propelled grenade. The young marine was airlifted to a base hospital, awarded a purple heart and eventually medically discharged. Giles prayed that John, who had exhibited signs of PTSD, hadn't taken his life like too many combat veterans.

He stared at the framed pen and ink and charcoal drawings of iconic buildings in major US cities lining the opposite wall. A beat passed as he contemplated whether he owed it to John or his family to reconnect with their past.

"Okay, Ms. Campos. I'll be there."

He could almost imagine the woman smiling when she said, "Thank you, Mr. Wainwright."

Giles hung up and slumped down in the chair. He had just come back from the Bahamas two days ago, and he was looking forward to sleeping in his own bed for more than a week and hopefully catch up on what was going on with his parents and siblings.

Most days found him working in his office hours after other employees had gone home. It was when he spent time on the phone with his Bahamas-based broker negotiating the purchase of several more uninhabited islands. Other days were spent in weekly meetings with department heads and dinner meetings in the company's private dining room with the officers and managers—all of whom were Wainwrights by bloodline or had married into the family.

Wainwright Developers Group was the second largest real estate company in the northeast, and everyone associated with the company was committed to maintaining that position or bringing them to number one.

Swiveling on his chair, he sent Jocelyn an email, outlining his travel plans for the following Thursday. Giles had no idea where Wickham Falls, West Virginia, was, but in another week he would find out.

Giles deplaned after the jet touched down at the Charleston, West Virginia, airport. A town car awaited his arrival. Jocelyn had arranged for a driver to take him to Wickham Falls. She had also called a hotel to reserve a suite because he did not have a timetable as to when he would return to New York.

The trunk to the sedan opened, and seconds later the driver got out and approached him.

"Mr. Wainwright?"

Giles nodded. "Yes." He handed the man his suit-case and a leather case with his laptop.

When he'd boarded the jet, Giles had experienced a slight uneasiness because he still could not fathom what he would encounter once he arrived. He had racked his brain about possible scenarios and still couldn't dismiss the notion that something had happened to John Foley.

He removed his suit jacket, slipped into the rear of the car, stretched out his legs and willed his mind blank. When Jocelyn confirmed his travel plans, she informed him that Wickham Falls was an hour's drive from the state capital. Ten minutes into the ride, he closed his eyes and didn't open them again until the driver announced they were in Wickham Falls. Reaching for his jacket, he got out and slipped his arms into the sleeves.

"I'm not certain how long the meeting is going to take," he said to the lanky driver wearing a black suit that appeared to be a size too big.

"Not a problem, Mr. Wainwright. I'll wait here."

Giles took a quick glance at his watch. He was thirty minutes early. His gaze took in Wickham Falls's business district, and he smiled.

It was the epitome of small-town Americana. The streets were lined with mom-and-pop shops all sporting black-and-white awnings and flying American flags. Cars were parked diagonally in order to maximize space. It was as if Wickham Falls was arrested in time and that modernization had left it behind more than fifty years before. There was no fast-food restaurant or major drug store chain. To say the town was quaint was an understatement.

He noted a large red, white and blue wreath suspended from a stanchion in front of a granite monument at the end of the street. A large American flag was flanked by flags representing the armed forces. Giles knew it was a monument for military veterans.

He strolled along the sidewalk to see if John Foley's name was on the monument. There were names of servicemen who'd served in every war beginning with the Spanish–American War to the present. There was one star next to the names of those who were missing in action, and two stars for those who'd died in combat. Although he was relieved not to find the corporal's name on the marker, it did little to assuage his curiosity as to why he had been summoned to Wickham Falls.

As he retraced his steps, Giles wasn't certain whether he would be able to live in a small town. He was born, grew up and still lived in the Big Apple, and if he wanted or needed something within reason, all he had to do was pick up the telephone.

He opened the solid oak door to the law firm and walked into the reception area of the one-story, salmon-colored stucco building. He met the eyes of the middle-aged woman sporting a '60s beehive hairstyle, sitting at a desk behind a closed glass partition. She slid it open with his approach. His first impression was correct: the town and its inhabitants were stuck in time.

"May I help you, sir?"

Giles flashed a friendly smile. "I'm Giles Wainwright, and I have an appointment at eleven to meet with Mr. McAvoy."

She returned his smile. "Well, good morning, Mr. Wainwright. Please have a seat and I'll have someone escort you to the conference room."

He nodded. "Thank you."

Giles did not bother to sit on the leather sofa, but stood with both hands clasped behind his back. He had sat enough that morning. First it was in the car heading for the airport, then all through the flight and again during the drive from the airport to Wickham Falls. He had altered his normal morning routine of taking the elevator in his high-rise apartment building to the lower level to swim laps in the Olympic-size pool.

Swimming and working out helped him to relax, while maintaining peak physical conditioning from his time in the military. Going from active duty to spending most of his day sitting behind a desk had been akin to culture shock for Giles, and it had taken him more than a year to fully adjust to life as a civilian.

"Mr. Wainwright?"

He turned when he recognized the voice of the woman who'd called him. "Ms. Campos."

The petite, dark-haired woman with a short, pixie hairstyle extended her hand. "Yes."

Giles took her hand and was slightly taken aback when he noticed a small tattoo with USMC on the underside of her wrist. He successfully concealed a smile. It was apparent she had been in the Marine Corps. *"Semper fi,"* he said sotto voce.

Nicole Campos smiled. "Are you in the Corps?"

He shook his head. "I proudly served for ten years."

"I was active duty for fifteen years, and once I got out I decided to go to law school. I'd love to chat with you, Mr. Wainwright, but you're needed in the conference room."

Giles always looked forward to swapping stories with fellow marines, yet that was not a priority this morning. He followed her down a carpeted hallway to a room at the end of the hall.

His gaze was drawn to a woman holding a raven-haired baby girl. Light from wall sconces reflected off the tiny diamond studs in the infant's ears. The fretful child squirmed, whined and twisted backward as she struggled to escape her mother's arms.

He smiled, and much to his surprise, the baby went completely still and stared directly at him with a pair of large round blue eyes. She yawned and he was able to see the hint of two tiny rice-like teeth poking up through her gums. He couldn't pull his gaze away from the baby girl. There was something about her eyes that reminded him of someone.

His attention shifted from the baby to the man seated at the head of the conference table. His premature white hair was totally incongruent to his smooth, youthful-looking face.

Giles smiled and nodded. "Good morning."

"Good morning. I'm Preston McAvoy. Please excuse me for not getting up, Mr. Wainwright, but I'm still recovering from dislocating my knee playing football with my sons." He motioned to a chair opposite the woman with the baby. "Please sit down."

Giles complied, his eyes meeting those of the woman staring at him with a pair of incredibly beautiful hazel eyes in a tawny-gold complexion. He wondered if she knew she looked like a regal lioness with the mane of flowing brown curls with gold highlights framing her face and ending inches above her shoulders. A slight frown appeared between her eyes as she continued to stare at him. He wondered if she had seen him during his travels in the Bahamas, while Giles knew for certain he had never met her because she was someone he would never forget; she was breathtakingly beautiful.

Preston cleared his throat and opened the file folder on the table. He looked at Giles and then the baby's mother. "I'm sorry when my assistant called to ask you to come in that she was bound by law not to tell you why you'd been summoned." He removed an envelope from the folder and withdrew a single sheet of paper. His dark eyes studied each person at the table. "This is a codicil to Samantha Madison Lawson's last will and testament."

Giles went completely still. The name conjured up the image of a woman from his past who had disappeared without a trace. Now it was obvious he had not come to West Virginia for an update about a fellow soldier, but for a woman with whom he'd had an off-and-on liaison that went on for more than a year.

"Ms. Lawson, before she passed away," Preston continued, "made provisions for her unborn child, hence named Lily Hope Lawson, to become the legal ward of her sister, Mya Gabrielle Lawson. Ms. Lawson, being of sound mind and body, instructed me not to reveal the contents of her codicil until a month following her death." He paused and then continued to read from the single page of type.

Giles, a former marine captain who had led men under his command into battles where they faced the possibility of serious injury or even death, could not still his momentary panic. A tense silence swelled inside the room when Preston finished reading.

He was a father! The woman sitting across the table was holding his daughter. He had no legal claim to the child, but his daughter's mother sought fit to grant him visitation. That he could see Lily for school and holiday weekends, Thanksgiving, Christmas and one month during the summer, while all visitations would have to be approved by Mya Gabrielle Lawson.

Giles slowly shook his head. "That's not happening." The three words were dripping with venom.

"What's not happening?" Preston questioned.

"No one is going to tell me when and where I can see my daughter."

"You've just been told." The woman holding the child had spoken for the first time.

Chapter Two

Mya was certain the rapid pumping of her heart against her ribs could be heard by the others in the room. She hadn't been able to move or utter a sound when the tall, black-haired man with piercing blue eyes in a suntanned face walked into the conference room. It had only taken a single glance for her to ascertain that the man was Sammie's ex-lover and Lily's father. He continued to glare at her in what was certainly a stare down. However, she was beyond intimidation because legally he had no claim over her daughter.

"That's where you're wrong," Giles countered in a low and threatening tone. "As Lily's biological father, I can sue for joint custody."

"If you do, then you will surely lose," Mya countered.

Preston cleared his throat. "I'm afraid Ms. Lawson's

right, Mr. Wainwright. Legally, you have no right to the child. But look on the bright side, because it was the baby's mother's wish before she passed away that you could have a relationship with your daughter."

Giles's eyes burned like lasers when he turned to glare at Preston. "You fail to understand that a woman carried my child and neglected to notify me about it. Even though she's gone, you're allowing her to become the master puppeteer pulling strings and manipulating lives from the grave?"

Preston shrugged shoulders under a crisp white shirt. "Ms. Samantha Lawson must have had a reason for not informing you about the baby. I'm going to leave you and Mya alone, and I suggest you work out an arrangement that you both can agree on. Please keep in mind it's what's best for the baby." Reaching for a cane, Preston rose to his feet and limped out of the office.

Lily began squirming again, and Mya knew it was time to feed her and then put her to bed. "We're going to have to put off this meeting for another time because I have to get home and feed Lily."

"I don't have another time," Giles said. "The sooner we compromise, the better it will be for all of us."

A wry smile twisted Mya's mouth. Spoken like a true businessman. She wanted to tell him it wasn't about compromising. The terms in the codicil did not lend themselves to negotiating a compromise. "That's not possible now because I'm going home."

"Then I'll go with you."

Mya went completely still, and she stared at Giles as if he had taken leave of his senses. Did he actually expect her to welcome him, a stranger, into her home as if she had offered him an open invitation? "You want to come home with me?"

He cocked his head at an angle. "I don't hear an echo."

Her temper flared. "You cocky, arrogant—"

"I know I'm an SOB," he drawled, finishing her outburst. "Look, Ms. Lawson," he continued in a softer tone. "Up until a few minutes ago I had no idea that I was a father. But if Samantha had told me she was carrying my child, I would've made provisions for her and the child's future."

Mya scooped the diaper bag off the floor and looped the straps over her shoulder. "In other words, you wouldn't have married Sammie, because you weren't ready for marriage and fatherhood. She wouldn't tell me your name, but she did open up about your views on marriage and children." Mya knew she had struck a nerve with the impeccably dressed businessman when he lowered his eyes. Everything about him reeked of privilege and entitlement. His tailored suit and imported footwear probably cost more than some people earned in a month.

"What's the matter, Mr. Wainwright? You see a little girl with black hair and blue eyes and suddenly you're ready to be a father? What happened to you asking for a paternity test?"

Giles's eyes narrowed. "I don't need a paternity test because Lily looks like my sister."

"If that's case, then you can save some money," Mya mumbled under her breath. Suddenly she realized she wasn't as angry with Giles Wainwright as she was with her sister. Sammie had completely blindsided her with the codicil.

Giles rounded the table and took the large quilted bag off Mya's shoulder. "Please let me help you to your car."

Mya resisted the urge to narrow her eyes at him. At least he'd said please. She walked out of the room, Giles following as she cradled Lily to her chest. Fortunately for her, the baby had quieted. She had parked the Honda Odyssey in the lot behind the office building.

Pressing a button on the remote device, she opened the door to the minivan and placed Lily in the car seat behind the passenger seat. She removed the baby's hand-knitted sweater and buckled her in.

"We'll be home in a few minutes," she crooned softly as Lily yawned and kicked her legs. She closed the door and turned around to look for Giles. He was nowhere in sight. Where could he have gone with the diaper bag?

"Are you looking for this?"

She turned to find him standing on the other side of the vehicle, holding the bag aloft. Bright afternoon sun glinted off his neatly barbered inky-black hair. Closing the distance between them, she held out her hand. "Yes. I'll take it now."

Giles held it out of her reach. "I'll give it back to you when you get to your house."

She didn't want to believe he was going to hold the bag hostage. Mya bit her lip to keep from spewing the curses forming on tongue. She wanted the bag, but more than that she needed to get her daughter home so she could change and feed her and then into her crib for a nap.

She knew arguing with the arrogant man was just going to delay her. "Okay," she conceded. "Follow me."

She flung off Giles's hand when he attempted to assist her into the van. The man was insufferable. She couldn't understand how Sammie was able to put up with his dictatorial personality. It was as if he was used to giving orders and having them followed without question.

Mya hit the start-engine button harder than necessary. Lily's father was definitely working on her very last frayed nerve. She maneuvered out of the parking lot, not bothering to glance up at the rearview mirror to see if he was following her.

Mya's fingers tightened around the steering wheel at the same time she clenched her teeth. She knew the anger and frustration she'd unleashed at the man who'd just discovered he was Lily's father was the result of Sammie keeping her in the dark as to her child's paternity; repeated attempts for her to get her sister to disclose the identity of the man who'd gotten her pregnant had become an exercise in futility. It was a secret Sammie had taken to her grave.

And why now? Mya mused. What did Sammie hope to prove by waiting a month after her death to disrupt not only her life, but also Lily's and Giles Wainwright's? She decelerated and took a quick glance in the rearview mirror to see a black town car following her minivan.

Giles closed his eyes as he sat in the back of the sedan. Samantha was dead and he was a father! What he found incredulous was that they'd never made love without using protection. And to make certain he would not father a child, Giles had always used *his* condoms, because he did not trust a woman to claim she was using birth control when she wasn't. And while he had been forthcoming when he told women he'd slept with that he wasn't ready for marriage and fatherhood, he never said he did not want a wife or children. It was just that the timing wasn't right, because after serving his country for ten years as a captain in the Marine Corps, he found difficulty transitioning to life as a civilian.

Giles opened his eyes and stared out the side window. Towering trees growing close to one another nearly blotted out the sunlight, while a series of waterfalls washing over ancient rocks had probably given the town its name. The mountainous landscape appeared untamed, forbidding. It was a far cry from the skyscrapers, crowded streets, bumper-to-bumper traffic and the sights and sounds that made his hometown so hypnotically exciting. He sat straight when the driver turned off into a long driveway behind Mya's minivan.

He leaned forward. "Don't bother to get out," he ordered the driver. "I'm not certain how long I'm going to be inside."

"I'll wait here, Mr. Wainwright."

Giles reached for the colorful blue-and-white-patterned diaper bag. He was out of the town car at the same time Mya had removed Lily from her car seat. The baby's head rested on her shoulder.

Looping the straps of the bag over one shoulder, he gently gathered Lily from Mya's arms. "I'll carry her." He met Mya's brilliant catlike eyes, not seeing any of the hostility she had exhibited in the law office.

"Thank you."

He followed her up the porch steps to a house he recognized as a modified Louisiana low-country home.

As a developer, he had gotten a crash course in architectural styles and he favored any residential structure with broad porches welcoming the residents and callers with cool shade. Tall shuttered windows and French doors were representative of the French Colonial or plantation style.

Admiring the house with twin fans suspended from the ceiling of the veranda, the white furniture, and large planters overflowing with live plants did not hold as much appeal as the small, warm body pressed to his chest. He lowered his head and pressed a kiss on her silky curls. The distinctive scent associated with babies wafted to his nose, a pleasing fragrance that reminded him of the times he'd held his nephews.

His previous declaration that he wasn't ready for fatherhood no longer applied, because the child in his arms was a blatant reminder that he had to get ready. He and Samantha engaging in the most intimate act possible had unknowingly created another human being. Even before sleeping together, he and Samantha had talked about marriage and children and he was forthcoming and adamant that he wasn't ready for either.

And when he'd walked into the conference room and had seen the infant for the first time, there was something about her that reminded him of someone, and within minutes of the attorney reading the contents of the codicil, Giles knew that someone was his sister. Lily had inherited Skye's raven-black hair and blue eyes. Giles, his mother, his sister and his cousin Jordan were the dark-haired anomalies among several generations of blond Wainwrights.

He watched Mya as she unlocked the front door; she tapped several buttons on the wall to disengage the house's security system. He stared at her delicate profile, wondering what was going on behind her impassive expression. She and Samantha may have been sisters, but there was nothing physically similar that confirmed a familial connection. Samantha had been a petite, curvy, green-eyed blonde, while Mya was tall, very slender, with a complexion that was an exact match for the gold strands in her chestnut curls.

She held her arms out for the baby. "I'll take her now."

Giles handed her the sleeping infant and then the bag. "What are you going to do with her?"

"She needs to be changed, and then I'm going to give her a bottle before I put her to bed."

A slight frown appeared between Giles's eyes. "It's lunchtime. Aren't you going to give her food?" he asked. Mya had mentioned having to feed her.

Mya shook her head. "No. I'll give her a snack after she wakes up. The bottle will hold her until then. Make yourself comfortable in the family room. I'll be back and then we'll talk about what's best for Lily."

Giles felt as if he had been summarily dismissed as he stared at Mya's narrow hips in a pair of black tailored slacks. He walked over to a pale-pink-and-white-pinstriped sofa and folded his tall frame down.

Everything about the space was romantic and inviting, beckoning one to come and sit awhile. He admired the floor plan with its open rooms, high ceilings and columns that matched the porch posts. French doors and windows let in light and offered an unobstructed view of the outdoors. Wide mullions in the off-white kitchen cabinet doors were details repeated in the home's many windows. The tongue-and-groove plank ceiling, off-white walls, kitchen cabinets, cooking island and breakfast bar reflected comfortable family living.

Family. The single word reminded him that he now had a family of his own. A hint of a smile tilted the corners of his mouth when he thought of his daughter. Then within seconds his smile vanished when he realized he had no legal claim to her. The lawyer had indicated Samantha was of sound mind and body when she drew up her will and then added the codicil, but Giles wondered if she actually had been in her right mind. It was obvious Samantha had died, and he wondered if she had known she was dying?

Giles knew he could challenge the will and authenticate his paternity. He had the resources to hire the best lawyers in the country to sue for sole or joint custody with Mya. Lily may be a Lawson, but she was also a Wainwright. And Giles wasn't above using his family name and wealth to claim what belonged to him.

He rose to his feet when Mya reappeared. She had exchanged her slacks and man-tailored blouse for a pair of skinny jeans and an oversize University of Chicago T-shirt. Thick white socks covered her bare feet. She had brushed her hair off her face and secured it in a ponytail. Giles found that he couldn't pull his gaze away from the small, round face with delicate doll-like features. He retook his seat after Mya sat opposite him on a chair.

"How old is Lily?" he asked; he decided he would be the one controlling the conversation.

"Seven months." Her eyebrows lifted slightly. "How well did you know my sister?"

Giles was taken aback by Mya's question. "What do you mean by how *well*?"

Mya crossed her arms under her breasts at the same time she crossed her outstretched legs at the ankles. "I know you were sleeping with her, but what else did you know about her?"

"Apparently not enough," he countered flippantly. "Maybe I was mistaken, but I thought she told me she was from a small town in Virginia, not West Virginia."

"You were mistaken because we've never lived in Virginia. What else do you know about her? Did she ever talk to you about her parents or her family?"

Giles cursed under his breath. He wanted to be the one to interrogate Mya, yet unwittingly she had turned the tables on him. "She told me her parents were dead, but nothing beyond that. Most times we talked about the places she had visited as a flight attendant, while I wasn't very forthcoming about my time in the military because I did not want to relive some of what I'd seen or done."

Mya's expression softened as she angled her head. "Were you deployed?"

He nodded. "I managed to complete a couple of tours in Afghanistan."

"Thank you for your service."

Giles nodded again. Suddenly he was reflective. Now that he thought about it, there wasn't that much he had known about Samantha Lawson, except that he enjoyed whatever time they had spent together whenever she had a layover in New York, which wasn't that often.

"Samantha and I did not spend a lot of time together," he admitted. "She would call me whenever she had a layover in New York and there were occasions when we'd just go out for dinner. She loved the theater, so if she had a few days to spare, I'd purchase tickets for whatever play she wanted to see."

"But you did sleep with her."

"Yes. And I always used protection."

Mya lowered her arms. "Sammie told me you did. But we both know the only form of birth control that is one hundred percent foolproof is abstinence."

A wry smile twisted Giles's mouth. "I'm fully aware of that now." He sobered. "You claim that you and Samantha are sisters, yet you don't look anything like her."

"That's because we were both adopted. Our parents couldn't have children, so they decided to adopt. They adopted me first, and then two years later they adopted Sammie. My sister spent all of her adult life searching for her birth mother and that's probably the reason why she wanted me to adopt Lily, so I would be able to tell her everything she would need to know about her mother. When she found out she was having a girl, she selected the name Lily Hope, after her favorite flower and Sammie's hope she would someday find her mother. My sister spent hours writing letters to her unborn baby and making recordings so Lily could hear her voice."

Sadness swept through Giles as he attempted to deal with all that his former lover had planned for their daughter. "Please answer one question for me, Mya?"

"What is it?"

"Did Samantha know she was dying?"

Mya averted her head. "Yes. When she discovered she was pregnant, she was also diagnosed with Stage IV breast cancer. Chemotherapy couldn't be given during throughout her pregnancy, so she had to wait until after the baby was born for radiation and hormonal therapy. However, during her second trimester she did undergo a mastectomy, but by the time she delivered Lily the cancer had spread to her liver and lymph nodes. Even though she never complained, I knew she was in pain. In the end, I hired a private duty nurse to take care of her because she refused to go to hospice. The nurse made certain to keep her comfortable, and several days after Lily turned six months old, Sammie passed away. And when she's older, I'll show Lily where her mother and grandparents are buried."

Giles felt as if someone had reached into his chest and squeezed his heart, making it nearly impossible for him to draw a normal breath. He hadn't found himself in love with Samantha, yet if he had known she was sick, he would have been there for her even if she wasn't carrying his child. "I'm so sorry."

Mya exhaled an audible sigh. "She's at peace now."

He leaned forward, hands sandwiched between his knees. There was something he had to know before he decided his next move and he hoped Mya didn't construe it as heartless. "Was Samantha of sound mind and body when she drew up her will?"

"Are you thinking of challenging her will because you don't believe she was in her right mind?"

"That's not what I'm saying," he argued softly.

"That's exactly what you're saying," Mya said in rebuttal. "There was nothing remotely wrong with Sammie when she drew up her will. She refused to tell me who had fathered her child, and I didn't understand her reasoning until Mr. McAvoy mentioned your name. Sammie did reveal that she was sleeping with a wealthy New York businessman, and when I finally heard the name Wainwright I understood her reluctance to tell me, because you probably would've talked her into having an abortion so as not to besmirch your family name when the word got out that you had a baby mama."

Giles covered his face with his hand, unable to believe what Mya was saying. "Is that what you really think?" he asked through his fingers.

"It's not what I think, but how Sammie felt. I know she withheld the fact that she had your child, but in the end she did redeem herself with the codicil. She didn't want Lily to spend her life looking for her father as it had been with her and her birth mother."

"What about you, Mya? Do you intend to raise Lily as your daughter?"

With wide eyes, she stared at him. "I *will* raise her as my daughter. I'm not only her legal guardian, but also her adoptive mother. I'm the only link between Lily's past and her future, so if you're thinking about suing me for custody, then I'm prepared to fight you tooth and nail for *my daughter.*"

Giles went completely still. He had underestimated Mya. There definitely was fire under her cool demeanor. "There's no need to fight each other when we both want what's best for Lily."

"And that is?"

"For her to grow up loved and protected."

"And you don't think I'll be able to love and protect her, Giles?" Mya asked.

He smiled. "I don't doubt you will, but she needs to grow up knowing she has a father."

"She will, because Sammie has granted you visitation."

"How many times a year? And don't forget a month in the summer."

"Being facetious will definitely not endear you to me, Giles."

"I don't intend to be facetious. I'm just repeating the terms of the codicil."

Mya closed her eyes. The verbal interchange was beginning to wear on her nerves *and* give her a headache. Not only was Giles strong-willed but he was also relentless in his attempt to undermine her sister's decision to conceal her pregnancy from him. The Wainwright name was to real estate as Gates was to Microsoft, and Samantha, knowing this, had attempted to make provisions for Lily that would prevent her from becoming a legal football between the Lawsons and Wainwrights.

"I'm not your enemy, but if you keep pushing me then I'll become your worst nightmare. I'm willing to grant you more liberal visitation than what Sammie stated in her will. And that means I'm not opposed to you taking Lily to New York to meet your family, but not without me. Wherever she goes, I go along."

"I don't have a problem with that."

Mya was mildly shocked he would agree to her terms. "You'll have to let me know in advance because she has scheduled doctor's appointments."

"What about you, Mya? What about your work schedule?"

"My schedule is flexible, because I'm now a stay-at-home mother. I resigned my teaching position once Sammie moved back home."

"What and where did you teach?"

"Comparative literature at the University of Charleston."

He mentally filed away this disclosure. "Do you miss teaching?"

"A little, but I love being with Lily." Mya didn't tell Giles that working at home allowed her to pen her novels in her spare time. "When are you going back to New York?"

A beat passed. "Tomorrow morning. Once I get back I'll have to rearrange my work schedule before I return. I'm going to give you several numbers where you'll be able to reach me. Jocelyn Lewis is my administrative assistant. So if you call my office, make certain you identify yourself and she'll put you through to me."

Mya stood, Giles also rising with her. "I'm going to get my phone so you can program your numbers into it."

Reaching into his shirt pocket, Giles handed Mya his cell phone. "You do the same with your contact info."

Her thumbs moved quickly over the keys as she tapped in her name, address, cell and landline numbers, along with her email address. She retrieved her phone from where she had left it on the dining room table and gave it to Giles.

"How many numbers do you have?" she asked when he took an inordinate amount of time tapping keys.

"Three. I'm giving you my cell, the number at the office, and the one in my apartment." Glancing up, he winked at her. "You can always send me a text if you need me for anything. And I do mean anything."

Mya stared, momentarily speechless. The warmth in his voice and the tenderness in his expression made her fully aware of why her sister had been taken with him. Not only was he urbane, but also unquestionably charming when he chose to be.

She smiled. "I'll keep that in mind if I do *need* you for something."

Giles returned Mya's phone to her. "I'll call you once I make arrangements to return. You don't have to see me out," he said when she made a move to walk him to the door.

Mya met eyes that shimmered like polished blue topaz. "Safe travels."

He inclined his head. "Thank you."

Giles settled himself into the rear of the car. He had revised his plan to remain in Wickham Falls for more than one day. Scrolling through his phone directory, he tapped Jocelyn's number. She answered after the first ring.

"I need you to arrange for a flight back to New York for tomorrow morning out of the regional airport." The regional airport was a shorter distance from his hotel. "And please call my mother and let her know I would like to see her tomorrow night at seven. Be certain to let her know dinner will be at my place."

"Consider it done."

"Thank you, Jocelyn."

He had asked Jocelyn to contact Amanda because Giles did not get to see his mother as often as she would like. Unlike her other son, Giles's position took him out of the country, and he wanted to tell her in person that she had another grandchild—and this time it was a girl.

And while he wanted to wait for Lily to wake up from her nap to see her again, he knew Mya needed time to accept that she would now have to share her daughter with him. Putting distance between them would also help him to try to understand why Samantha had elected not to tell him about the baby.

Had she viewed him as someone who had used her for only for sex? Did she not trust him to take care of her and the baby? Or had she denied him his parental rights because she knew he had been adamant about not wanting to marry or father a child?

There was one more person he wanted to call, but he decided to wait until after he checked into the hotel.

If Samantha hadn't told him about the baby, then he wondered if there were other things she'd sought to conceal from him. Not only did he intend to have Samantha's background dissected but also her sister's. And if anything negative about either of them surfaced, then he was prepared to bring holy hell down on Mya to secure full custody of his daughter.

Chapter Three

Giles settled into a hotel suite less than an hour's drive from a regional airport. After checking in, he changed into a swimsuit and swam laps in the indoor pool. Once he had showered and changed into a pair of walking shorts and a rugby shirt, he ordered room service.

A ringtone on his phone indicated a text message from Jocelyn:

Return flight scheduled for departure at 1:00 PM tomorrow at Tri State Airport. Ground transportation confirmed. Confirmed dinner with your mother

Giles responded with: Thank you.

He could always count on Jocelyn to simplify his life. Once he had set up the company's international division, Giles couldn't convince his older brother to run the department with him. Patrick had declined because, as a husband and now a father of two young boys under the age of six, he claimed he didn't want to be away from his family even if it was only for a week.

Patrick also professed he preferred working with their father in the legal department to jetting off to exotic climes, leaving Giles to ponder how much longer he would be able to maintain a one-man operation. Several third-generation Wainwrights cousins were still undecided whether to come and work for the company. He had made them generous offers to come and work with him, yet they still were ambivalent about becoming involved in the real estate business.

He finished his lunch and left the tray on the floor outside the door. Walking across the room, he flopped down on the king-size bed and reached for the cell phone on the bedside table and dialed the number to Jordan's cell phone. It rang four times before going directly to voice mail. He decided not to leave a message. Either Jordan was in court or with a client. He made another call, this time to his cousin's office.

Jordan had always teased Giles, declaring they were the family outsiders. Jordan and his law school mentor had gone into partnership, setting up Chatham and Wainwright, PC, Attorneys at Law. The firm was housed in a brownstone in Harlem's Mount Morris Park Historic District. Despite his reputation as a brilliant corporate attorney, Jordan refused to work for the family business, while Giles had opted for the military rather than join the company once he'd graduated college.

"Good afternoon, Chatham and Wainwright. How may I direct your call?"

"I'd like to speak to Jordan Wainwright."

"May I ask who's calling?"

"Giles Wainwright."

"Hold on, Mr. Wainwright. I'll see if he's available to take your call."

"Thank you." He didn't have to wait long before he heard Jordan's familiar greeting.

"What's up, G?"

Giles smiled. Jordan was the only one in the family who referred to him by an initial. "I'd like to hire your firm to conduct a background check on a couple of people." A swollen silence followed his request.

"Why are you asking me when your legal department can do it?"

"I'm asking you because what I'm going to say to you should stay between us. Attorney-client privilege," he added.

"What's going on, Giles?"

He knew he had gotten Jordan's attention when he addressed him by name. Giles was completely truthful when he told Jordan everything—from sleeping with Samantha, the phone call asking him to come to Wickham Falls, West Virginia, and to the revelation that he was now the father of a seven-month-old little girl and the rights extended to him as her father.

"That's really a low blow," Jordan drawled.

Giles smiled in spite of the seriousness of the situation. "I agree. I need to know everything about Samantha Madison Lawson and Mya Gabrielle Lawson. Both were adopted, so I don't know how far back you'll be able to go."

"I'll have the investigators begin with their adoption records and go forward from there. Is there anything you've noticed about the aunt that would make her unfit to be your daughter's mother?"

"Not really. We spent less than an hour together. Her home is clean and tastefully furnished, and she claims to have taught college-level literature."

"Does she appear financially able to raise and educate the child until she is emancipated?" Jordan asked.

Giles stared up at the ceiling. "I don't know. That's what I need for your people to find out." Although Mya drove a late-model vehicle, it wasn't in the luxury category. He also had no idea if Samantha had life insurance, and if she did, if Mya had been her beneficiary. His concern was how she was supporting herself as a stay-at-home mother.

He had called Jordan because he knew he would never divulge what Giles had just told him. However, Giles knew he owed it to his parents—his mother in particular—to let her know that they had another grandchild.

"Are you prepared to accept the results if they come back clean?"

"I'll have to accept it, but that doesn't mean I'm going to stop fighting to claim my daughter."

"I wouldn't expect you to give up," Jordan continued, "because I would do the same if I were in a similar situation. What I wouldn't do is antagonize your daughter's mother. Try to remain civil with her and perhaps she'll come around and allow you more involvement in the baby's life."

"That's what I'm hoping will happen." Giles paused. "Do I have an alternative if the background checks yield nothing? What can I use to sue for at least joint custody?"

"Your only other option would be charging her with neglect. You'll have to be able to prove that the child has failed to thrive, that she doesn't get the medical care she needs, or if you've witnessed any verbal or physical abuse. I've never handled a child abuse or neglect case, but Aziza has. Although she's well versed in the family court system, I don't want to involve her in this because she's so close to her due date. Maybe after the baby's born and if she feels up to it, I'll ask her to look into this for you."

"When is she due again?"

"October 5. The doctor says the baby could come a week before or a week after that date."

"You still don't know if you're having a girl or a boy?"

"No. We want to be surprised."

"Have you narrowed it down to names?"

"We're leaning toward Maxwell if it's a boy and Layla if it's a girl."

"I like those names."

His cousin and his wife were given the privilege of selecting names for their unborn baby, while he'd had no say in naming his daughter. Every time he thought about Samantha's deception, it served to refuel his anger.

"Look, G, I'm going to hang up because I have a client waiting for me. And don't worry about the background checks. I'll have the investigators get on it ASAP."

"Thanks, Jordan."

"No need to thank me. Talk to you later."

Giles ended the call and rested his head on folded arms. He would take Jordan's advice and not do anything to antagonize Mya because she held all of the cards when it came to Lily's future. At least for now.

What she wasn't aware of was his intent to use any and everything short of breaking the law to claim his daughter.

The following evening Giles opened the door to his apartment and waited for his mother to emerge from the elevator.

Amanda Wainwright stepped out of the car, her smile indicating she was as pleased to see him as he was her. It was a rare occasion when Giles saw his mother without a fringe of hair sweeping over her ears and forehead. Tonight she had styled her chin-length, liberally gray-streaked black hair off her face. She was conservatively dressed in tailored taupe slacks she had paired with a white tailored blouse. She was hardly ever seen in public without her ubiquitous navy blazer, Gucci loafers and the magnificent strand of South Sea pearls and matching studs she had inherited from her grandmother.

There had been a time after graduating college and before he'd joined the marines when they had rarely spoke to each other. However, that changed when Giles called to inform his mother he was being deployed to Afghanistan. After all, he'd owed it to her to let her know he would be going into combat.

That single call changed him forever. It had taken days before he could forget the sound of her heartbreaking sobs. He apologized for severing all communication with her, while she apologized for interfering in his life and attempting to control his future. He returned to the United States after his first tour, shocking his parents when they opened the door to find him in uniform grinning ear to ear. The homecoming signaled a change in their relationship. He was still their son, but he had also become a decorated war veteran.

"Hello, gorgeous."

An attractive blush suffused Amanda's fair complexion with the compliment. Giles had been truthful. His mother's stunning beauty hadn't faded at sixty-four. It was her tall, slender figure, delicate features, coal-black hair and vibrant violet-blue eyes that had attracted Patrick Wainwright II, who married her after a whirlwind courtship; a year later, they had welcomed their first child.

Amanda rested a hand on Giles's light stubble. "You are definitely your father's son. You always know what to say to make a woman feel good."

Giles kissed her forehead. "You have to know by now that I never lie." He threaded their fingers together and led her through the foyer and into the expansive living-dining area.

She pointed to the dining area table set for two. "You cooked?"

He seated his mother on a love seat and dropped down next to her. "Surely you jest," he said, smiling. His many attempts to put together a palatable meal had resulted in either over- or undercooked dishes that always ended up in the garbage. In the end, he preferred eating in or ordering from his favorite restaurants or gourmet shops.

"I ordered from Felidia. It should be here in about twenty minutes."

Amanda gave Giles a long stare. "Why did you order in? You know I love eating there because the place reminds me of a little ristorante Pat and I discovered when we were in Bologna."

"I decided we'd eat in because I need to talk to you about something."

"Please don't tell me you're going to rejoin the military."

Giles dropped an arm over his mother's shoulders and hugged her. "No. What I want to tell you shouldn't be disclosed in public."

Amanda's eyelids fluttered as the natural color drained from her face. She rested a hand over the pearls. "Please don't tell me something that's going to hurt my heart."

He shook his head. "It's something you claim you've been wishing for. You now have a granddaughter."

Giles knew he had shocked his mother when her hands trembled, but then she quickly recovered and cried tears of joy. Waiting until she was calmer, he told her everything he'd disclosed to Jordan. He left out the fact that he wanted his cousin to conduct a background check into the lives of his daughter's mother *and* adoptive mother.

Amanda sniffled as she opened her handbag and took out several tissues. "What are you going to do?" she asked, after blowing her nose.

"I'm going to take the legal route to claim my daughter."

"You claim you have visitation, so when can we expect to meet her?"

Giles recalled the designated holidays outlined in the codicil. "It probably won't be until Thanksgiving."

A crestfallen expression crossed Amanda's face. "That's more than two months from now."

"I know, Mom. I'm hoping to convince Mya to bring her before then."

"Who else knows about this?"

"Just you and Jordan," he admitted.

Amanda rested her head on her son's shoulder. "I'd rather not say anything to Pat right now, because he's probably going to go ballistic and go after this poor girl who had no idea what her sister was planning."

Giles pressed a kiss to his mother's hair. "You're right." There was nothing his father liked better than a legal brouhaha. "Then this will remain between you, me and Jordan for now." The chiming of the building's intercom reverberated through the apartment. "That's probably our dinner."

He answered the intercom. The doorman announced a delivery from Felidia. "Please send them up."

Two hours later, Giles escorted his mother to the street, waited for her to get into a taxi and stood on the curb watching as it disappeared from his line of vision.

It was as if he could exhale for the first time in more than twenty-four hours. Talking to his mother, and her decision not to tell her husband temporarily assuaged his angst over attempting to explain the circumstances of him becoming a father.

Giles shook his head to rid his thoughts of the possible scenarios Patrick could employ to make Lily a Wainwright, because he intended to use his own methods to get what he wanted. If he was able to get a judge to rule in his favor to grant him joint custody, then he would happily comply with the law to share his daughter with Mya.

The sidewalks were teeming with locals and tourists in sweaters and lightweight jackets to ward off the early autumn chill. Giles, not wanting to return to his apartment, walked along Second Avenue to Forty-Second Street, stopping at intervals to do some window-shopping before reversing direction and heading back uptown. The walk had been the antidote to release some of his anxiety about reuniting with Mya and hopefully agreeing to what was best for Lily.

The night doorman stood under the building's canopy. "Have a good evening, Mr. Wainwright."

Giles nodded and smiled. "You do the same, Raoul."

During the elevator ride to his floor, Giles mentally mapped out what he had to accomplish before returning to Wickham Falls. He knew it was time for him to give Jocelyn more responsibility if he was going to be away for any appreciable length of time. And that meant she would have to accompany him during his next trip to the Bahamas.

Mya sat on the porch, bouncing Lily on her lap. Giles had called to inform her he was in Wickham Falls and for her to expect him to arrive at her house before one that afternoon.

It had been three weeks since their initial meeting, and she had resigned herself to accept him as Lily's father. If Sammie hadn't wanted her daughter to have a relationship with her father, then she never would've added the codicil.

She had gotten up earlier that morning to put up several loads of laundry, give Lily breakfast and followed with a bath. After dressing her, she spent fifteen minutes reciting nursery rhymes. Mya knew Lily was more than familiar with many of the words and would be able to repeat them once she began talking.

Her daughter had become quite a chatterbox when she babbled about things Mya pretended to understand, while their favorite games were patty-cake and ring around the rosy. Now that Lily was standing up while holding on, Mya would gently pull her down to the floor when she sang the line "they all fall down" in "Ring Around the Rosie."

Mya went completely still when she registered the sound of an approaching car. The vehicle maneuvering up the driveway wasn't a town car but an SUV with New York plates. And as it came closer, she noticed a car seat.

Mya held her breath when Giles got out and waved to her. He looked nothing like the well-dressed man who had questioned her late sister's decision not to grant him custody of their daughter. Relaxed jeans, a sweatshirt with a fading USMC logo and running shoes had replaced the business attire.

She rose stiffly, as if pulled up by a taut overhead wire, and waited for his approach. He hadn't shaved and the stubble afforded him an even more masculine quality.

At first, she had asked herself why her sister had put up with him, but seeing him like this, Mya realized Giles Wainwright was not a man most women could ignore at first glance. Piercing blue eyes and balanced features made for an arresting face. He was tall, several inches above six feet, broad-shouldered and appeared in peak physical condition.

Giles slowly made his way up the porch steps, stopping only a few feet from her.

"Hello again."

An unconscious smile parted Mya's lips. "Welcome back. How long do you plan to stay?"

Giles met her eyes. "I don't know. It's open-ended, so I checked into an extended stay hotel."

Her smile faded. "What do you mean by open-ended?"

"I may have to go to New York for a few days for meetings, but once they're concluded I'll be back.

Her jaw dropped. "Oh I see."

"Hopefully you do, because it's going to take a while for Lily to get used to seeing me, so I'm prepared to take as much time as necessary to bond with *my daughter*."

His reference to Lily being his daughter was not lost on Mya. Biologically the baby was his daughter, but legally Lily was hers. "I'm not opposed to you bonding with *my* daughter," she countered, smiling. "And if there is anything I can do to speed up the process, then please let me know."

She knew she had shocked him with the offer when he gave her a long, penetrating stare. It was apparent he hadn't expected her to be that cooperative. His gaze shifted to Lily.

"May I hold her?"

"Hold out your arms and see if she'll come to you."

Giles extended his arms, and much to his surprise Lily leaned forward and held out her arms for him to take her. He smiled at the little girl looking up at him. "She looks different from when I last saw her." Her hair was longer and there was a hint of more teeth coming through her upper gums.

Mya leaned against the porch column and crossed

her arms under her breasts. "I'm able to see her change even though I'm with her all the time. Right now she's teething, so she's drooling on everything." As if on cue, Lily picked up her bib and gnawed on it.

Giles shifted his attention from Lily to Mya. He marveled that a woman without a hint of makeup and wearing faded jeans and a white T-shirt and socks could appear so incredibly sensual.

"How old is she now?"

"She turned eight months two days ago."

He quickly did the math. "Her birthday is February 5?"

"Yes."

"Our birthdays are four days apart. Mine is February first."

"That's quite a coincidence." Mya turned and opened the storm door at the same time Lily let out a piercing scream. "That's her way of telling me she wants to be changed. In fact, it's time for her afternoon nap."

Giles followed Mya inside the house and sniffed the air. "Something smells good."

Mya glanced at him over her shoulder. "I'm making pot roast. You're more than welcome to stay for dinner."

He stared at the denim fabric hugging her hips and smothered a groan. Giles knew it wasn't going to be easy to completely ignore the woman with whom he would spend time whenever he came to see Lily. Everything about her turned him on: her face, body, hair, softly modulated voice with a hint of a drawl and then there was the way she stared at him. It was as if she knew what he was thinking or going to say before he spoke.

Jordan had come up with nothing—not even a parking ticket—in Samantha and Mya's background for him to use as leverage to bolster his case if and when he decided to sue her. The only alternative was to watch for signs of neglect, and watching Mya closely was definitely going to become a delightful distraction.

"I'd like that very much. Do you cook every day?"

"Yes, because I have to prepare meals for Lily."

Giles slipped out of his running shoes, left them on the thick straw mat near the door and followed Mya through the living room and up a flight of stairs to the second story. "You don't buy baby food from the supermarket?"

"No. I've heard stories about jars of baby food being recalled because of foreign objects, so I decided it's safer and healthier to prepare her food myself. I'll cook carrots, beets, spinach or sweet potatoes and then purée them to a consistency where she can swallow without choking."

"That's a lot of work."

"She's worth it." Mya stood at the entrance to the nursery. "Do you want to change her?"

Giles didn't mind holding a baby but usually drew the line when it came to changing diapers. The few times he'd changed his nephews it was apparent he had been too slow when they urinated on him. "I'll watch you do it."

Her eyebrows flickered a little. "You've never changed a baby?"

"Only boys. My brother has two sons." Giles handed her Lily.

"The fact that they're not anatomically the same shouldn't make a difference. You are familiar with the female body, aren't you?"

Giles narrowed his eyes. "That's not funny. I remember you warning me about being facetious," he added when she gave him a Cheshire cat grin.

She scrunched up her nose. "I do remember saying something like that."

Giles had to smile. His daughter's mother was a beautiful sexy tease. How different she was from their first encounter where he could feel her hostility. This was a Mya he could readily get used to.

"Everything you'll need to change her is in the drawers of the changing table." She opened and closed each drawer. "Here are diapers, wipes, lotion and plastic bags for the soiled diapers."

He stood at the changing table positioned at the foot of the crib and watched as Mya removed Lily's bib and onesie. She quickly and expertly changed the wet diaper and disposed of it in a plastic bag. "Where do you put the plastic bag?"

"There's a garbage can in the mudroom."

Giles studied the exquisite furnishings in the nursery. It was apparent Mya had spared no expense when it came to decorating the space. Green and pink were the perfect contrast for the white crib, dresser and chest of drawers. The colors were repeated in the rug stamped with letters of the alphabet with corresponding images of animals. A solid white rocking chair and footstool had covered cushions in varying shades of pink and red roses.

"Is she sleeping throughout the night?"

Mya nodded. "Now she is."

"What time do you put her to bed?"

"Eight."

He angled his head. "That should give you a few hours for yourself before you turn in for the night."

"A few," she said cryptically. Mya handed Lily back to Giles. "You can hold her while I throw away the diaper and bring up a bottle."

Giles smiled as Lily stared up at him with curious, round, clear blue eyes with dark blue centers. "Hello, princess. I'm your daddy and now that I'm here we're going to get to see a lot of each other. I have lots of plans we can do together once you're older. I'm going to teach you to swim, ice-skate and, when the time comes, how to drive. You like sports?" he asked, continuing his monologue with the little girl. "Well, if you're a Wainwright, then you'll definitely be into sports. And if you come to live with me in New York, then you're going to have to decide whether you like the Yankees or the Mets. Those are baseball teams. You don't have to choose when it comes to football because your cousin Brandt played for the NFL. That means we always cheer for one of the New York teams. Rooting for the Rangers rather than the Islanders is a better pick since you'll be living in Manhattan. Let's see, what's left? Oh! I forgot about basketball. Your daddy is partial to the Knicks, although I also like the Nets.

"Then there's your family. Your birth certificate may list you as Lawson, but I don't want you to ever forget that you are a Wainwright. You'll probably be a little overwhelmed when everyone will want a piece of you, but not to worry because Daddy will make certain to take care of his princess. And when you're older and you want to live with me in New York, I'll make it happen. There's a wonderful school blocks from Central Park where several generations of Wainwrights were educated."

"Don't, Giles."

He turned to find Mya standing in the doorway to the nursery. "Don't what?"

"Don't promise her things that may not become a reality. I know she doesn't understand what you're telling her. And I forgot to tell you that Sammie's will states that Lily should be raised here."

Giles clenched his teeth in frustration. It was apparent Mya wasn't that ready to compromise, that she was going to hold to Samantha's mandate that Lily grow up in a town where the residents appeared reluctant to accept it was now the twenty-first century.

"Do you realize how manipulative your sister was? That she's controlling three lives from the grave?"

Mya reacted as if he had struck her across the face. "Maybe she had a reason for setting up the conditions for how she wanted her daughter to be raised."

"What reason could that be?" Giles spat out, angrily.

"I don't know, because I wasn't aware that my sister was seeing someone until after she'd become pregnant. And even then she refused to tell me your name."

"I think we need to talk."

"What about?"

"About my relationship with your sister."

"You are so right about that," Mya said.

Giles handed Lily to Mya and stalked out of the room. If Samantha hadn't revealed the name of her baby's father, then he had to assume she had never spoken to Mya about him or their on-again, off-again liaison.

He knew he could never move forward in his quest

to claim his daughter if he withheld the truth about the woman who had remained an enigma even before she disappeared from his life.

Chapter Four

Mya found Giles in the family room. He stood with his back to the French doors. "Are you going to stand while we talk?" she asked.

He took several steps and pointed to the love seat. "You first."

She sat and he folded his tall frame down on a chair opposite her. "Where and how did you meet my sister?"

Stretching out long legs, Giles stared at his sock-covered feet. "Samantha was the flight attendant assigned to first class on my flight from the Bahamas to the States. I had a connecting flight in Miami, but all planes were grounded because of severe thunderstorms. I decided to check into a hotel rather than spend hours in the airport waiting for the weather to clear. Samantha and several crew members were checking into the same hotel because they weren't scheduled to fly out again until the following day. She invited me to have drinks with her, and we agreed to meet in the hotel lounge."

"Are you saying that Sammie picked you up?"

Giles shook his head. "No, she didn't. We'd passed the time during the flight from Nassau to Miami chatting about movies, so when she suggested we have drinks, I accepted because I'd found her pretty and outgoing. She told me her parents were dead and that she was an only child. When I mentioned her Southern drawl, she said she'd grown up in a small town in what I'd assumed was Virginia."

Mya bit her lower lip to still its trembling. She wondered how many other men had Sammie told the same lie. "Why do you think she lied to you?"

Giles lifted broad shoulders under his sweatshirt. "I don't know."

"What else did she tell you?"

"She said she hated growing up in a small town and that's why she decided to become a flight attendant. And when I asked her what she wanted for her future, she claimed she hadn't figured that out. When the topic of marriage and children came up, we both agreed we definitely weren't ready for either." Giles paused, seemingly deep in thought. "After seeing her a couple of times, whenever she had a layover in New York I could detect restlessness in her. As if she was always looking for something or someone. And when I mentioned it to her, she played it off, saying she always felt more comfortable in the air than on the ground."

Mya had to agree with Giles when he talked about Sammie being restless. "That someone she was looking for was her birth mother." She told him about Samantha's mother getting into a taxi with her week-old baby and when she got out, she hadn't bothered to take the infant with her. "There were times when I suspected Sammie never really appreciated what our adoptive parents did for us. She'd complain about feeling incomplete because she'd been abandoned."

"I suppose her feeling that way wouldn't permit her to engage in a committed relationship."

Mya stared at Giles. "You wanted a commitment from her?"

He blinked slowly. "I wanted more than her calling me every couple of months to tell me she was in town and wanted to see me."

Mya frowned. "So you just wanted to see her for sex?"

"No! There were times when we were together and never made love. I'd always ask her when I would see her again because she knew her flight schedule well in advance, and her answer was 'I don't know.' We dated off and on for a little more than a year, and then it ended. One month passed and then another and after the third month, I knew it was over."

"Had you argued about something that made her angry?"

"We may have had some minor disagreements but it never escalated to an argument. Come to think of it, I did notice she would become sullen whenever I talked about my family."

"That's because you grew up with your biological mother and father and she didn't."

He sat straight. "So she punishes me by having my child and using her as a pawn so I'll never be able to legally claim her as a Wainwright."

A shiver of annoyance snaked its way up Mya's spine. She wasn't about to let Giles attack her dead sister. "Maybe because you are a Wainwright Sammie feared you would use your family's name and money to take Lily away from her because you'd told her you weren't ready for marriage and fatherhood. In other words you'd take the baby but not the mother."

"I'm not going to lie and say I was in love with your sister, but I'll say it again that if I'd known she was carrying my baby, I definitely would've provided for them."

Mya threw up a hand. "Do you hear yourself, Giles? You talk as if money will solve everything. Sammie didn't need money because our parents made certain we would be financially secure before they passed away. They left us this house and their furniture-manufacturing company, which we sold because neither of us wanted to get involved in running a business. Sammie had two life insurance policies, and as the beneficiary I invested most of the monies in tax-free bonds for Lily's college education and whatever else she'll need to start life on her own."

Giles ran a hand over his face. "None of this makes sense."

Mya closed her eyes when she recalled the times when they recited their prayers before going to bed, and Sammie's prayer was always the same. She wanted to find her real mother. Those were the times when Mya resented the Lawsons for telling Sammie she was adopted. It would've been so easy for them to say she was their biological daughter because of the physical resemblance. But living in a small town where it was difficult to hide anything made that virtually impossible.

She opened her eyes. "It doesn't make sense because you have what Sammie wanted most in life. My sister used to spend hours on the computer pouring over sites dedicated to people searching for their relatives. She told me whenever she had a layover in the Midwest she would search through local birth and death records for a woman who'd given birth to an infant girl around the time she was born. Sammie couldn't know where she was going because she didn't know where she had come from."

"Where did her mother abandon her?"

"It was in New Lebanon. It's a city southwest of Dayton, Ohio."

"What about you, Mya? You've never searched for your birth mother?" Giles asked.

"No. Because whoever she is, I know if she'd been able to take care of me she wouldn't have left me in the hospital. When people ask me about my race, I always tell them I'm African-American. And if they asked whether I'm mixed race, my comeback is, isn't everyone? All they have to do is take the ancestry DNA test to find their true ethnicity."

Giles laughed. "That is so true."

Mya realized it was the first time she'd heard Giles laugh. The sound was low and soothing. "Sammie did take a DNA test and it said she had ancestors who were European Jewish, Russian and Scandinavian. She focused on the Scandinavians because they'd settled in the Midwest."

Giles angled his head and smiled. "I guess that makes Lily quite an ethnic gumbo."

He sobered. "I'm glad you told me about Samantha. I think I understand her a little better now."

"Are you still upset that she didn't tell you about Lily?"

"Whether I'm upset is irrelevant. What's done is done. What you and I have to do is come to an agreement as to what is best for Lily. You have a jump on being a mother while I have to learn that being a father is a lot more than offering financial support. I will not make any decisions concerning Lily unless I discuss it with you. I did tell my mother that she has a granddaughter, so she's anxious to meet her."

"What about your father?" Mya asked.

"He still doesn't know, and Mom and I won't tell him until you're ready to come to New York."

"What if we aim for Thanksgiving?" Mya knew it was one of the holidays Sammie had designated for visitation, yet after talking with Giles she was willing to be flexible as long as he didn't threaten or put pressure on her about Lily's future.

"That'll work. That gives us at least six weeks to get used to being a family."

Mya wanted to ask Giles about his relationship with his father when she recalled his statement about fatherhood: *I have to learn that being a father is a lot more than offering financial support.*

Had his father not been a positive role model? Had he just provided financial support while relinquishing the responsibility of child rearing to his wife? She'd heard the expression *more money, more problems.* Did his father's wealth did not translate into knowing or doing what was best for his progeny?

Mya pushed to her feet. "Where are my manners? I forgot to ask you if you wanted lunch."

Giles rose in one fluid motion. "Thank you for offering, but I had a buffet breakfast before I left the hotel." He glanced at his watch. "It's time I go and check in with my office." He winked at her. "By the way, what time is dinner?"

"Six."

"I'll see you later, Mya."

Mya nodded. "Okay."

She watched as he slipped into his shoes, walked out of the house and closed the self-locking door. Giles's arrival had altered her writing schedule. She had to tweak a proposal for the next book in her series and submit it to her editor by the end of the week.

When her sister came back to Wickham Falls with the news that she was staying until she delivered her baby, Mya knew her well-ordered life would never be the same. Before Sammie's return, all she had to concern herself with was refining her lectures notes; reading and grading papers and penning novels in her spare time. And now when she had adjusted to being a full-time mother and part-time writer, she would now have to change again. This time she would have to adapt to sharing Lily with Giles.

Fortified with a cup of fresh pineapple and a cup of green tea, Mya raced up the staircase and into the office to see how much she could accomplish before Lily woke up.

Giles noticed the blinking light on the hotel phone; there were only three people who had the number for the hotel: his mother, Jordan and Jocelyn. He'd sent Jordan a text with the number to avoid Mya overhearing their conversations if the call came through his cell. He smiled. Jordan had left a message for him to call him back.

"Hey, brand-new Daddy. Are you getting any sleep?" he asked Jordan.

"Barely. My boy really has a set of lungs. He's hungry all of the time and I've told Aziza to give him a bottle in between breast feedings."

"What did she say?"

"I can't repeat it on an open line. She says she wants to breastfeed him until he starts cutting teeth. Not to change the subject, but what's going on down there with Mya?"

"So far it's all good," Giles admitted. "She seems to have softened her stance about coming to New York with me."

"When is she coming?"

"She mentioned Thanksgiving. Hopefully she'll change her mind and we'll come sooner. I found out that she doesn't need money, so that's an argument I can't use as a basis for joint custody." He told Jordan about Mya's parents leaving her and her sister the house and business. "The baby is getting bigger and more delightful than when I first saw her."

"So you like being a daddy?"

Giles smiled. "I'm getting used to it. What I really want to be is a hands-on father. I want to be there for her piano and dance recitals. I want to become involved during parent-teacher conferences and—"

"Enough, G," Jordan said, interrupting him. "I know you resent your father not being there for you because he put WDG ahead of his family obligations. Think about it, Giles. The company is a python. It constricts and then swallows you inch by inch until you can't get out. Don't be like Patrick. Take time to enjoy your family before it's too late."

"I will." He paused. "And thanks for the pep talk."

Jordan laughed. "There's no need to thank me. You've helped me get my act together more times than I can count. Now, the next time we talk, I want you to tell me that you and your baby's mother have become one happy little family."

"We'll see," Giles said noncommittedly. "Give Aziza my love and kiss Maxwell for me."

"Will do," Jordan said.

After ending the call, Giles thought about his cousin's reference to one happy little family. That had become a reality for Jordan when he married Brandt's attorney. They were now the proud parents of a little boy. He knew Jordan wasn't just blowing smoke when he talked about taking time to enjoy being part of a family. Jordan and his law partner agreed he would take a six-week paternity leave. Six weeks.

And that's how long Giles planned to stay in Wickham Falls, and hopefully when he left to return to New York it would be with Mya and Lily.

Leaning back in the desk chair, he studied a framed print of a beach scene. The suite was a cookie-cutter replica of many others he'd checked into. While some suites were more luxurious and opulent, the overall physical design was the same. He compared the furnishings with those in the villas on the islands owned by WDG International. With the assistance of his broker, WDG, Inc., sold several properties to the wealthy looking to live permanently on their private island, while several others were designated as vacation properties.

Reaching for the television remote, he turned on the television and began channel surfing. Viewing what he sometimes referred to as mindless TV had become the distraction to temporarily take his mind off his work. Occasionally he would get out of bed in the middle of the night to boot up his computer to input ideas for a new project, aware that he had become his father.

Patrick Wainwright II rarely shared the evening meal with his family. He left home at dawn to go into the office and occasionally returned home after everyone had retired for bed. The running family joke was when had Pat found the time to get his wife pregnant—not once or twice, but three times?

In the past, Giles never would've stayed out of his office for more than a week. Now it would be six weeks. And he was prepared to stay in Wickham Falls even longer if he was able to convince Mya that it was in his daughter's best interest to connect with her other family.

Legally, Lily was Mya's daughter, while biologically she was his. And that made her their daughter and a family.

Holding Lily against his heart and feeling the warmth of her little body had elicited an unconscious craving to protect her against everything seen and unseen.

Giles stood on the porch, peering through the glass on the storm door. He rang the bell and within seconds Mya came into view carrying Lily on her hip. Smiling, she unlocked and opened the door.

"You're early."

He kissed her cheek. "I thought I'd come by and see if I can help with something."

His admiring gaze swept over her face, lingering on her mouth, before slowly moving down to a loose-fitting light blue blouse and navy leggings. A pair of blue ankle socks covered her feet. The first time he'd come to the house, he'd noticed Mya did not wear shoes indoors. It was obvious she was a neat freak because everything was in its place and the floors were spotless.

"Should I take off my shoes?"

"Please. Only because Lily's crawling and she puts everything she finds on the floor in her mouth. I should've warned you that jeans and sweats are the norm around here, because Lily will sometimes spit up her food or milk."

Bending slightly, he took off his slip-ons, leaving them on the mat beside her running shoes. "I'll know for the next time." He'd exchanged his jeans and sweatshirt for a dress shirt and slacks.

"Did you come to help me cook?" Mya asked.

Giles stood straight. "I can't cook. I came to baby-sit." He reached for Lily who extended her arms for him to take her. He pressed his mouth to her hair. "Hi, princess."

Mya stared at him as if he'd spoken a foreign language. "How do you eat?"

"I order in or I eat out."

"You're kidding me, aren't you?"

"No, I'm not. I never learned to cook. I can make coffee and toast, but not much beyond that."

Mya shook her head and rolled her eyes upward. "That's pitiful."

"What's pitiful?"

"What if you can't order in or go out? Do you subsist on toast and coffee?"

Giles winked at her. "I always have peanut butter on hand."

She smiled. "You're hopeless. Come with me to the kitchen. I have to finish making Lily's dinner."

"Should I close and lock the door?"

"You can if you want."

"Do you always leave the inner door open?"

Mya nodded. "Most times I do. Of course I close and lock it at night. Why do you ask?"

"I don't like that you live here by yourself, while your closest neighborhood is across the road."

"I always keep the storm door locked. And my closest neighbor happens to be a deputy sheriff. He'll occasionally come over to check on me and Lily."

Giles sat on a stool at the cooking island and settled Lily on his lap. "I only asked because a woman living alone can become a target for someone looking to take advantage of her." His protective instincts had surfaced, and he did not want to think of something happening to Mya or Lily.

"There's no need to worry about us," Mya said.

"I have to worry about you and Lily." What Giles didn't say was that he now regarded both of them as family, and to him family was everything.

Mya washed her hands in one of the stainless steel sinks and then dried them on a towel from a stack on the quartz countertop. "I have a security system that's wired directly to the sheriff's office, and whenever someone rings the doorbell I see their image on my cell phone. Lastly, I have a licensed handgun and shotgun in the house, and I know how to use both."

"Damn!" he whispered under his breath. "You're a regular Annie Oakley."

"Please watch your mouth," Mya chided. "Lily may be too young to talk, but she does have ears. And d-a-m-n," she said, spelling out the word, "sounds too much like dada."

"Sorry about that. I suppose I don't spend enough time around children."

"Don't forget that you have a daughter and my pet peeve is a girl with a potty mouth."

"You don't curse?"

"I try not to. It comes from my upbringing. My Southern Baptist mama would have a fit if any of us used bad language."

Giles glanced around the ultramodern, all-white kitchen with bleached pine cabinetry and antique heart-of-pine flooring.

"Your home is exquisite inside and out."

"Thank you. I loved growing up here. It was somewhat of a culture shock when I moved to Chicago to attend college. I'd rented a one-bedroom apartment and I always felt as if the walls were closing in on me."

"You didn't like Chicago?"

"Please don't get me wrong. I loved the city, but I wasn't used to apartment living."

Giles digested this information. It was apparent Mya would be opposed to living in New York City, despite him owning a spacious two-bedroom condominium with incredible views of the East River and the many bridges linking Manhattan with other boroughs.

"How long did you live there?"

"Seven years. I stayed long enough to earn an undergraduate, graduate and post-graduates degrees."

Giles whistled, the sound causing Lily to look up at him. "That's a lot of learning."

"It was necessary because I wanted to teach college-level courses." Her head popped up and she gave him a direct stare. "Are you an architect?"

"No. I'm an engineer. I've familiarized myself with different architectural designs since becoming a developer."

"You build in New York?"

"No. I build in the Bahamas."

Her hands stilled. "You must spend a lot of time there because you're quite tanned." She went back to slicing a beet. "I hope you're using sunblock."

Lines fanned out around his eyes when he smiled. "I didn't know you cared," he teased. "And you sound like my mother."

Her smile matched his. "That's because mothers know best." She placed the carrot and beets in a blender. "How long have you been doing business in the Bahamas?"

"Four years."

Giles told her about leaving the military to join his family's real estate company. He set up the international division after he convinced the board to extend the monies he needed to purchase three undeveloped private islands. He subsequently hired an architect to design villas and worked with an engineer to build desalination processing systems to convert ocean water for human consumption. The sale of the islands yielded a three-hundred-percent profit for the company, and he was given the green light to purchase more uninhabited islands. He now headed the division to expand their holdings to build vacation resorts on private islands throughout the Caribbean.

Mya gave him an incredulous stare. "How many more have you bought?"

"We now own twelve. But only half have been developed."

"Are there that many islands up for sale?"

"The Caribbean Sea has an archipelago of about seven hundred islands and at least twenty-five hundred cays."

"That's amazing. I never could've imagined there would be that many."

He smiled. "What's amazing is there's an extensive list of millionaires and billionaires waiting to write checks so they can own an island."

"What specs should I look for if I wanted to buy an island?" Mya asked Giles.

"Acreage, and if it's an island with a beach. Some buyers want one that is turnkey or if it has income potential. Another important factor is access. They want to know if it has an airstrip or the capability for a fly-in."

"What's the price range, from high to low, for these rich folks' playgrounds?"

He smiled. For some owners, it was a private playground. "An island of about seven hundred acres will cost about sixty-two million. A smaller one measuring two acres will go for a quarter of a mil."

"Going, going, gone," Mya intoned, grinning. "I'll take the one with two acres."

"That's two acres with nothing on it. It'll probably set you back several million to make it habitable."

She affected a sad face. "Sorry, but I'm forced to withdraw my bid due to lack of funds."

Giles caught Lily's hand when she reached for his face. "Whoa, princess. Not the eye."

"You have to be careful with her because she likes pulling hair and gouging eyes. I try to keep her fingernails cut to minimize the damage."

"Maybe she's training for the baby WWE."

"That's not nice, Giles."

"What's not nice is her trying to put my eye out." He pretended to bite on the tiny hand as he watched Mya press a button on the blender. Within seconds, the beets and carrots took on a pinkish shade. She continued blending until the vegetables were converted into hot soup. She poured it into a small bowl to let it cool.

"That's remarkable. You just made hot soup in a blender."

"Vitamix isn't your ordinary blender. It doubles as a blender and food processor. I use it to make baby food, soups, smoothies, and frozen desserts." Mya opened a drawer under the cooking island and took out a bib. "You can put her in the high chair so I can feed her."

Giles took the bib from Mya and tied it around Lily's neck. "I'll feed her. I have to learn some time," he added when she shot him a questioning look. He placed Lily in the chair and carried it over to the breakfast bar.

"I'll finish putting dinner together while you feed your princess."

"Does it bother you that I call her princess?" he asked Mya.

She made a sucking sound with her tongue and teeth. "Of course not. Not when her mother is the queen."

It took him several seconds to understand her retort. He wasn't certain whether she was teasing him, and if she was then he wasn't offended. He preferred the teasing Mya to the one who occasionally radiated hostility. He understood her apprehension that he would attempt to challenge her right to his daughter, and Giles knew it would take time before she would trust him enough not to disrupt her life or Lily's. "If you are a queen, then what does that make me?"

"A king." She held up a hand when he opened his mouth. "Our monarchy will differ from most because as king and queen we will rule as equals."

"That sounds fair to me."

"So you're willing to learn to cook?"

"Oh…" Giles swallowed an expletive. "Do I have to?"

"Yes. I'll not have you filling Lily up on processed foods because you can't put together a healthy meal. Do you want your daughter plagued with high blood pressure and elevated cholesterol levels before she's enrolled in school?"

"Damn, woman," he said sotto voce. "You really know how to pile on the guilt."

"What did I tell you about cussin'? Do I have to put out a swear jar and charge you five dollars for every time you cuss?"

"I thought it was cursing, not cussin'."

"You're in the South, so down here it's cussin'."

He executed a mock bow. "Point taken, Miss Sweet Potato Queen."

Mya stared at him and then doubled over in laughter. His laughter joined hers and seconds later Lily let out a cackle and waved her hands above her head.

Even before their laughter faded Giles was filled with an overwhelming emotion shaking him to the core. He, Mya and Lily had become a family in every sense of the word. He was a father, Mya a mother and Lily was their daughter.

Chapter Five

Mya glanced over at Giles as he attempted to feed Lily. Although the vegetable soup had cooled enough for it not to burn her mouth, Lily continue to fret.

"Why is she crying?" he questioned when her whimpers became a loud wail.

"You're not feeding her fast enough."

"You're kidding?"

"No, I'm not."

"But…but won't she choke?"

Mya set down the potato ricer. "It's puréed, Giles." She walked over and took the spoon from him. "Let me show you." She made quick work of feeding the baby, who hummed and rocked back and forth with each mouthful. "It's like eating ice cream. You taste and then swallow."

Giles's dark eyebrows slanted in a frown. "I can't believe you make it look so easy."

"That's because I know what she wants. Do you want to try feeding her dessert?"

He nodded. "I can't give up now."

Mya retrieved a jar of a peach-and-pear mix from the refrigerator and gave it to Giles. She gave him a reassuring pat on the back. "Give yourself a couple of days and you'll be a pro."

She went back to ricing potatoes, adding cream, salt, pepper and garlic butter, then whisked the potatoes until they were smooth and fluffy. She'd made them as a side dish for the fork-tender pot roast. The slow cooker, Dutch oven and pressure cooker were her favorite kitchen appliances, and she alternated utilizing all three when preparing one-pot meals.

"Hooray! We're finished!" Giles clapped his hands while Lily joined him, putting her tiny hands together.

Mya blew them a kiss. "I told you you'd get the hang of it."

Giles proudly pushed out his chest. "What now?"

"Wet a paper towel and wipe her face. She always drinks water after her meals. Please get the playpen from the family room and put her in it. I'll get her sippy cup for you."

Mya filled a cup from the fridge in-door water dispenser and handed it to Giles. She knew it would take a while for him to become familiar with the routine she had established to meet her own and Lily's needs. There were mealtimes, bed, nap and playtimes. In between, she set aside time for grocery shopping, laundry, housecleaning and preparing meals.

Time had become a precious commodity and she jealously guarded the little she had for herself.

Giles placed Lily on the floor, watching as she crawled over to a stool and attempted to pull herself up by holding on to the legs. He moved quickly when the stool tipped precariously, catching it before it toppled over. Now he knew why Mya told him to put Lily in the playpen. He put her back in the high chair, retrieved the playpen and placed it between the kitchen and dining area. Lily took several sips from the cup before tossing it aside and redirected her attention to gnaw on the gel-filled teething ring, as she babbled what sounded like *mumum*.

Giles walked over to Mya and rested a hand at her waist. "I don't know how you do it."

She tilted her chin, staring up at him, and he suddenly found himself drowning in pools of green and gold. His eyes moved slowly over her high cheekbones. He smiled when she lowered her eyes, and charming him with her demure expression.

"Do what?"

"Take care of Lily, cook and keep the house clean."

"I'm no different from other mothers, whether they stay-at-home or work outside the house. We do what we have to do to keep from being overwhelmed."

Giles splayed his fingers over her back. "Don't you know some young woman looking to make some extra money, willing to come in and help clean the house?"

"I really don't need anyone to help me clean the house. There's only me and Lily, so aside from dusting, vacuuming and cleaning the bed and bathrooms, there's not much to do. I get a lot done when Lily's sleeping."

"What's going to happen when she doesn't sleep as much?"

"By the time she's five, I'll enroll her in kindergarten."

"Do you plan to go back teaching once she's in school?"

"If I do, then it has to be locally. I'll apply for a position at the high school. All of the schools in the Johnson County school district occupy the same campus, which makes it convenient for teachers and staff whose children are enrolled there."

He leaned closer and inhaled the lingering scent of Mya's perfume. Giles felt her go stiff and then relax against his hand. "So you have it all figured out as to Lily's future."

"No, I don't. If you want to eat, then you're going to have to let me go. I need to take the pot roast out of the slow cooker. Thank you," Mya whispered when he dropped his hand.

Giles wanted to tell her that if he had a choice between eating and touching her, he would've chosen the latter. He felt more comfortable and relaxed around Mya than he had with any other woman he'd met or known. At first, he'd contributed it to her connection to Lily but after spending time with her, he realized it was the woman herself.

There were so many things he admired about her but it was her sense of loyalty that had won him over. She had willingly sacrificed her career to care for her terminally ill sister and raise her niece. And she had become the perfect mother when she put Lily's needs above her own.

Jordan had revealed that his investigators had not

come up with anything in regard to a man or men in her life. There was no record of her having been married or divorced. And he wondered if she'd been involved with a man before she resigned her position at the college to become her sister's caretaker and Lily's adoptive mother.

Giles thought of Mya as a superwoman as she quickly, with no wasted effort, put dinner on the table. Along with the pot roast, carrots au jus, garlic mashed potatoes, an escarole salad with orange and grapefruit sections and red onions tossed with red wine vinegar, she also included corn bread and pitchers of chilled water and sweet tea.

"Oh my goodness," he crooned after swallowing a forkful of potatoes seasoned with a subtle hint of garlic and rosemary. "These potatoes are to die for." He raised his glass of tea. "I'm ready to enroll in cooking school."

Mya smiled. "When do you want to start?"

"What about tomorrow?"

"Okay. If you come early enough, I'll show how to prepare a traditional Southern breakfast with grits, sausage or bacon, with eggs and biscuits."

"What about lunch?"

"Lunch will be dinner leftovers. We'll vary it with pulled beef sliders. I've put away some of the mash potatoes and gravy for Lily's lunch."

Giles glanced over at Lily in the playpen biting on a rubber duck as he took a sip of sweet tea. Mya told him she preferred agave to sugar to sweeten the beverage. "What do you plan for dinner?"

"Chicken with a brown rice pilaf."

"Who taught you to cook?"

"I'm proud to say it was my mother. Mama earned a reputation as being one of the best cooks in the county. Whenever there was a church potluck dinner or PTA fund-raiser, her pies and cakes were the first to go. I used to come home after school and sit in the kitchen to do homework so I could watch her cook. The year I celebrated my twelfth birthday, she allowed me to assist her—but only on the weekends. Mama refused to let anything come before our schoolwork. She wanted me and Sammie to have careers—something she regretfully gave up after she married my father. She'd gone to college to become a math teacher but wound up keeping the books for Daddy's company after the longtime bookkeeper retired."

Giles listened, transfixed when Mya revealed how much her mother resented spending hours in an office above the factory floor tapping computer keys and writing checks. After twenty years in a childless marriage, she convinced her husband to adopt a child. Graham Lawson finally gave in and they adopted Mya.

"Before my adoption was finalized, Mama had trained a high school graduate to replace her, and at the age of forty-five, she finally become a mother. Then they adopted Sammie and years later, Mama told me that she'd felt complete for the first time in her life. By the time Mama was finally an empty nester, her perfect world crumbled when Daddy called her to say he was working late, but when he didn't come home, she called the foreman and asked him to go by the factory to check on him. They found him slumped over his desk. An autopsy concluded that he'd died from a massive heart attack."

Mya's eyelids fluttered. "Mama kept saying she had nothing to live for, while I tried to reassure that she still had her girls. Less than a year after Daddy passed, Mama died in her sleep. The doctor claimed it was heart failure, but I knew she'd died of a broken heart. She was an incredible mother and I'm certain if she was still alive she would be a spectacular grandmother."

Giles pushed back his chair and rounded the table when Mya's eyes filled with tears. He eased her up and pulled her into his arms. Everyone she loved was gone: mother, father and sister. He buried his face in her hair. "Your sister and parents are gone, but you still have a family. You have Lily."

She nodded. "I know that." Mya lifted her chin and met his eyes; her eyes were shimmering pools of green-and-gold tears.

"I promise to stay in this relationship for as long as it takes for Lily to grow up and walk across the stage at whatever college she chooses to accept her degree."

"Please don't make promises you're not certain you'll be able to keep."

Giles's hands moved up and cradled her face. "I never make a promise I can't keep."

Her hands covered his. "What if you meet a woman, fall in love and want to—"

Giles placed a thumb over her mouth, stopping her words. "Don't say it, Mya. Lily doesn't need a step-mother when she has you."

"You've lost your mind if you believe I'm going to agree to a twenty-year relationship with you just so we can raise Lily together."

His lips twisted into a cynical sneer. "What's the matter, Mama? Are you hiding a secret lover?"

A noticeable flush suffused her face with his gibe. "If I had a lover, I definitely would've married him within days of discovering you were Lily's father, because you showed your hand when you threatened to sue me for custody. And marrying the son of a local family court judge would've definitely stacked the cards in my favor."

"You were engaged?"

The seconds ticked as Giles held his breath and waited for Mya's response. How, he chided himself, had he been so self-absorbed that he hadn't considered perhaps there had been a man in Maya's life? After all she was the total package: looks, brains and poise—everything a most men would want in his woman. And he was no exception.

Mya lowered her eyes. "No. I was seeing someone for a while, but we broke up when I had to take care of Sammie."

"Why did you break it off?"

"I wasn't the one who ended it. He didn't believe me when I told him that my sister was ill. Even before that, we were seeing less and less of each other. A few times he'd go off on a waitress who'd mix up his order, or he'd exhibit uncontrollable road rage because he'd believed another driver had cut him off, and when I tried to tell him that he needed to seek counseling to manage his anger he'd accuse me of not having his back. After a while, I realized I didn't want to deal with his explosive temper and told him it was over. Four months later, he called to tell me he was in counseling and wanted to see me again. We went out a few times, but that's after Sammie returned to the Falls to tell me she was pregnant. When I told him about Sammie, he accused me of using her as an excuse to see other men. He hung up and I never heard from him again."

"Where does he live?"

"Charleston."

Giles brushed his mouth over Mya's slightly parted lips. "He's far enough away so you don't have to run into him. And if he bothers you, then he'll have to deal with me, and that's something I don't think he'd want to do."

She blinked slowly. "What would you do?"

"You don't want to know."

"I don't like violence, Giles."

"I don't, either," he retorted, "but I'm certainly not going to cut and run if he bothers you."

"Now you sound like a former marine."

"Wrong, baby. Once a marine, always a marine. One of these days I'll tell why I enlisted the Corps instead of going to work for the family business."

Lily let out a loud shriek and Giles and Mya turned to find her standing up while holding onto the mesh netting covering the sides of the playpen. "Mumum," she repeated over and over as she jumped up and down on the thick padding.

"What is she saying?" Giles asked Mya.

She shook her head. "I don't know. Usually when she wants me to give her something, she'll open and close one hand and say it. She's probably trying to say *me*."

"When is she going to start talking?"

"That all depends on the child. Some kids talk early and others wait until they're almost two and then speak in complete sentences. Lily is a chatterbox, and I'm sure that when she begins, she'll never stop."

"How about walking?"

"Now that's she pulling up and holding on, I'm willing to predict she'll be walking by herself by the time she's ten months." Mya glanced at the clock on the microwave. "It's almost time for her bath. I usually sit in the rocking chair and read to her before putting her in the crib."

Giles stared, complete surprise on his face. "You read to an eight-month-old?"

"Don't look so shocked. Haven't you heard about pregnant women reading or playing classical music for their unborn child?"

"No."

"Well, there are studies that prove that these babies usually are more alert and display more creativity than those who don't receive the same stimulation."

"What do you read to her?"

"Nursery rhymes and Dr. Seuss. It's the repetition that will make it easy for her to recognize certain words."

Giles angled his head and smiled. "That's why you're the teacher and I deal with putting up buildings while focusing on quarterly earnings and profit margins."

"Well, Mr. Hotshot Businessman, it's time I clear the table and clean up the kitchen. You can hang out with Lily until I take her upstairs for her bath."

Giles sat on a stool in the bathroom watching as Lily sat in the bathtub splashing water. Mya knelt on a fluffy mat and drew a washcloth over Lily's face and hair. She claimed it was only a sponge bath and the warm water helped Lily to relax. Once the baby was dressed for bed, Mya cradled Lily in her arms and rocked back and forth while reading *Goodnight Moon*.

He suddenly realized there was much more to parenting than writing checks to the orthodontist or tuition for private schools and colleges. It went beyond providing clothes, food and shelter. It was about nurturing and making a child feel loved. And it was the love that was priceless. He'd led men and women into combat and found that easier than being a father. His heart turned over when he saw Mya kiss Lily's head before placing her on her back in the crib.

She checked the locks on the windows and switched on a baby monitor and then placed a finger over her mouth and motioned for him to follow her. Mya flipped the wall light switch, and the night-lights plugged into several outlets provided enough illumination to move around the room without bumping into objects.

"She's down for the night."

Reaching for Mya's hand, Giles cradled it gently. "It's amazing how calm she was when you were reading to her."

"I think she likes the sound of my voice."

Giles wanted to tell Mya that her voice had a wonderful, soothing quality that he never tired of listening to. He silently applauded Samantha for choosing Mya to raise her child. He knew if he'd known of the pregnancy and his former lover had agreed to list him as the father on the birth certificate, he would've asked his mother to help him raise his daughter.

However, there were things a woman in her sixties wouldn't be able to do for an infant that a thirty-something woman could accomplish with ease. Amanda had raised three children with little or no input from her husband, and Giles knew it wouldn't be fair to ask his mother to take on the responsibility of raising her granddaughter.

They descended the staircase together. "I'm going to be on my way so you can have some time for yourself."

Mya laughed softly. "A man can work from sun to sun, but a mother's work is never done."

He squeezed her fingers. "I'm a witness to that." Mya walked him to the door where he retrieved his shoes. "What time do you want me to come tomorrow morning?"

"Eight o'clock is good. By that time I've fed and bathed Lily."

"Do you want me to bring anything?"

She smiled. "No, thank you. I have everything I need."

Giles knew he was making small talk because he didn't want to leave Mya—not yet. He wanted to end the evening sitting on the porch and enjoying the silence. It was something he'd found himself doing whenever he returned to his condo. He'd sit in the dark, staring out the window at the buildings across the river. That had become his time to get in touch with himself, to be still and listen to the beating of his own heart, while asking why he had survived when so many he'd known hadn't.

It was also when he questioned his purpose in life. He knew there was more than buying and selling private islands to those to whom price was no impediment. And it was when he realized he didn't see his mother, brother and sister often enough. That he spent too many hours in the office or in the air. His main concern was buying and selling land, while conferring with his Bahamian real estate broker Kurt De-Grom to work another deal. Lily had changed his life and his priorities. His daughter was now first and foremost in his life.

Resting his hands on Mya's shoulders, he leaned down and brushed a light kiss on her cheek. "Good night, my lady."

Her teeth shone whitely when she smiled. "Good night."

Mya closed and locked the door behind Giles before he drove away. She exhaled slowly as she made her way into the kitchen. It felt as if she could draw a normal breath for the first time since she opened the door earlier that morning to Giles's ring. Being around him made her feel as if his larger-than-life presence sucked up all of the oxygen in the room.

She'd always believed she had a monopoly on confidence, but interacting with Giles had her doubting herself, although he hadn't exhibited any of the hostility from their first encounter. It was as if she was waiting for the proverbial other shoe to drop. Whatever she had shared with Giles was still too new for her to lower her guard and trust him enough to let him into *her* life.

Mya knew how important it was for a girl to grow up with a father because Graham Lawson had become her father in every sense of the word. Whenever he came home, he'd called out for his girls. She and Sammie would race and jump into his arms while he spun them around and around until they pleaded with him to stop. Once they grew too tall and heavy and he more frail with age, they were resigned to a group hug.

She missed her parents but missed Sammie even more, because they were inseparable when growing up.

Their mother had given each girl her own bedroom, yet night after night, Sammie would come into Mya's room and crawl into bed with her. She claimed she was afraid to sleep alone because she was afraid of the dark. But even after Veronica installed night-lights in her younger daughter's bedroom, Sammie continued to come into Mya's room.

Sleeping together ended after Veronica offered them the opportunity to decorate their rooms because they were becoming teenagers. Along with the new furniture, each room had its own television, audio components and worktables for their computers and printers.

Sleeping separately signaled a change in Sammie, who had begun to spend most of her free time online searching for her mother.

Mya thought it eerie that her niece would share the same fate as her biological mother. As Veronica had chosen and loved her, Mya would make certain to let Lily know she had made the choice to love and raise her as her own.

Mya knew she should be in her office writing instead of sitting in the kitchen ruminating about the past as she recalled a course she had taught covering the works of D. H. Lawrence. There was something about Giles that reminded her of the characters in Lawrence's novella *The Fox*, where she compared herself and Lily to the author's Jill Banford and Nellie March, two females who live alone, while Giles was Henry Grenfield, a young man who comes to stay with them. Although Henry's presence was more psychological than physical, in the end the lives of the two females would never be the same.

Is that what's going to happen to us? Mya thought. She prayed that she had made the right decision to not only invite him into her home, but also allow him to share Lily's life as well as her own.

Chapter Six

It had taken two weeks, and the doubts Mya had about Giles proved unfounded when he seemed genuinely interested in not disrupting her life as he bonded with Lily. He was a quick study when it came to changing, bathing, dressing and feeding her, yet balked and complained that cooking involved too many steps and he didn't have the patience for measuring countless ingredients. When she reminded him that he was an engineer and had to utilize math, he said he had no interest in learning the differences between thyme, cilantro, parsley or dill. To him, they all were green leaves that did not taste the same. Mya knew it was useless to try to convince him and did not mention it again.

She had put Lily in her crib for her nap when she found Giles waiting for her in the hallway outside the nursery. He had taken her advice to wear jeans and

T-shirts because he liked rolling around on the floor with Lily whenever he pretended he was a cat or dog, barking, meowing, sniffing or nibbling on her toes.

"Is something wrong?" she asked, averting her eyes from the laser-blue orbs that suddenly made her feel as if he was undressing her. It was the first time that she felt physically uncomfortable with him. She come to look for his chaste kisses when he greeted her in the morning and before leaving at night because she felt there wasn't anything remotely sexual in his motives.

"If you don't mind my asking, I'd like to know where you disappear to when Lily takes her afternoon naps."

She took his hand. She knew he was curious when she declined to join him on the porch or in the family room. "Come with me and I'll show you." Mya led him down the hall to her office. Pushing open the door, she stepped aside to let him peer in. "This is where I write."

Giles entered the room Mya had set up as a home office. Floor-to-ceiling shelves spanning an entire wall were tightly packed with books. An L-shaped workstation positioned under one window held an all-in-one computer. Framed photographs of Samantha and Mya at various ages and with their parents crowded an oak drop-leaf table. Rays of afternoon sunlight reflected off the pale green walls and dark jade carpet.

His gaze lingered on a window seat large enough for two people to lay side by side. The fabric on a love seat matched the pink-and-white floral window-seat cushions. The office had everything one would find in a break room: watercooler, portable refrigerator, a single-cup coffee maker, radio and a wall-mounted flat screen television.

He noticed a stack of pages with red-penciled proof-reader notations. "Are you an aspiring writer?"

"Not any longer."

"You're published?"

Mya laughed when he gave her a look mirroring disbelief. The woman with whom he found himself more entranced each passing day continued to astound him. There was nothing about Mya with which he found fault. Even when he'd explained he honestly had no interest in learning how to cook, she did not press him. A lifting of her shoulders communicated *suit yourself.*

"Yes."

"What do you write?"

Mya dropped his hand and selected a paperback from several on a lower shelf, handing it to him. "New adult. This is my latest novel. It will go on sale next week."

He read the back cover of the novel. It was part of an exciting new series featuring a team of twentysomething cyberspace cold-case crime solvers. "Congratulations! That's a mouthful of alliteration," he said, smiling. "How did you come up with the plot?"

"I grew up reading books from my mother's childhood, and her personal favorite was Nancy Drew. I was still in grad school when I overheard several forensic science and prelaw students discussing a mock cold case their professor had assigned the class. I recalled details of their conversation whenever I watched the Investigation Discovery channel for episodes of *Disappeared*, *Snapped*, or *True Crime*. After a while, I'd filled several notebooks with what I'd gleaned from those shows.

"I'd planned to write a novel once I retired, so in my head, the project had become my plan B. Once I joined the faculty at the University of Charleston, plan

B kept nagging at me. I'd come home every night and write and before I knew it, I'd completed a novel. I created my team of cold-case crime solvers with five protagonists, three guys and two girls, who bond in a chat room but never meet in person. Once they become a crime-fighting team, they interact with one another by video conferencing, Skyping or with Face-Time. There's some subtle flirting between one guy and girl despite both being in committed relationships. I've gotten tons of email asking me to have them meet in person, but I'd like to keep their sexual tension going for a few more books."

"You must have an incredible imagination."

"It comes from being an avid reader. As a kid, I'd read any and everything. I'd sit at the breakfast table and read the cereal boxes. I read to Lily because I want her to grow up with her asking me to buy her a book rather than the latest video game."

Giles silently applauded Mya for introducing Lily to books before she could walk or talk. "How many books have you published?"

"Six. I recently submitted a proposal for the next two titles in the series." Mya told him how she'd arbitrarily selected the name of a literary agent from the internet and mailed off a letter outlining her proposed series. It took nearly five months before she got a reply with a request for Mya send her the completed manuscript. She continued to write, finishing two more novels, when she finally received a call from her agent informing her that an editor from an independent New York publisher wanted to publish her series.

Giles continue to stare at the cover. "If you're a *USA Today* bestselling author, why are you using a pseudonym?" It listed her as Hera Cooper. It was definitely the reason Jordan's investigators hadn't discovered she was also a published author.

"I'd thought it best that my students didn't know their professor was moonlighting as a writer."

"Why Hera Cooper?"

"Cooper was my mother's maiden name and Hera was the supreme Greek goddess of marriage and childbirth and had a special interest in protecting married women. She was also Zeus's wife and sister, but that's another story."

"That is creepy."

"There was a lot of creepy stuff going on in Roman and Greek mythology."

Giles dropped a kiss on her curls. "One of these days I want you to give me a crash course on mythology. I never could get the names of the gods straight. I'm ashamed to admit English wasn't one of my best subjects, and that's why I took every elective math and science course available to boost my GPA."

"Where did you go to college?"

"MIT."

"Impressive!"

Giles buried his face in her fragrant hair. He liked seeing Mya with a cascade of curls framing her face. "The University of Chicago is right up there with MIT."

"Yeah, right."

Hugging Mya and kissing her good-morning and good-night seemed as natural to him as breathing. It just happened involuntarily. He pulled back and turned to face her. "You're beautiful and brilliant." He noticed the flush darkening Mya's face with the compliment. "Do you have any idea how incredible you are?"

She lowered her eyes. "I'm far from being incredible."

"Self-deprecating, too?" he added with a wide grin. "The day the book debuts, we'll have to go out and celebrate. The problem is there aren't too many fancy eating establishments around here."

Mya chuckled. "Ruthie's is as fancy as we get here in the Falls. It's an all-you-can-eat, buffet-style family restaurant."

Giles curved an arm around her waist. "I'd like to take you to someplace more upscale with tablecloths, a waitstaff and an extensive wine list."

"We'd have to go to Charleston if you really want fine dining. One of my favorites is The Block Restaurant and Wine Cellar. But if you want exceptional Italian food, then Paterno's at the Park is the place to eat. My other favorite is The Chop House, which has earned a reputation for serving some of the best aged steaks in the state."

"Choose the one you want and I'll call and make reservations."

Mya rested her head on his shoulder. "Have you forgotten we have a baby and no sitter?"

Giles groaned aloud. "I forgot about Lily. I suppose we'll have to wait until we get to New York where my mother will babysit her while we go out or…"

"Or what?" Mya asked.

"What if we don't wait until Thanksgiving to go New York?"

"What are you talking about?"

"Why don't we—you, me and Lily—go to New York now? We can introduce her to my immediate family before the remaining hoard of Wainwrights gather for

Thanksgiving. We can also celebrate the release of your book at the same time. Perhaps you'd even want to drop in and see your editor."

"I did enough celebrating with the release of my first title when I drank four glasses of champagne and woke up the next day with a dry mouth and pounding head-ache. Sammie sent me a gift of a week's vacation at an all-inclusive resort in the Dominican Republic. She surprised me when she showed up on the second day. We hung out on the beach during the day and danced all night until we dropped from exhaustion."

There was silence for a moment, and then Mya spoke again. "That was one of the happiest times in our lives. It was as if we hadn't a care in the world. There are times when I still don't believe she's gone. I miss her just that much." Going on tiptoe, she buried her face in the hollow of Giles's throat. "Forgive me for being such a Debbie Downer.

"It's okay, baby. I miss her, too."

Giles's hands circled her waist, molding their bodies together. He tried to ignore the crush of her full breasts and failed when the flesh between his thighs stirred to life. He'd told himself that Mya was off-limits because he had slept with her sister, but the silent voice in his head reminded him they were sisters in name only.

Suddenly Giles felt as if he was on an emotional roller coaster, because if anyone would have hinted more than a year before that he would be a father he would've said they were crazy. He'd told Samantha that he wasn't ready to have children, but now that Lily was here he had to ensure his daughter's future, and that meant a relationship with the child's mother.

He had committed to stay connected to a woman for

the next twenty years so they could raise their daughter together, a woman who hadn't given him the slightest indication she wanted anything more than friendship. And at this point in his life he wasn't certain whether he wanted more than friendship from Mya. And if he did, then it would have to be because of her and not because she's was Lily's mother.

"There are times when I think I hear her voice even though I know it's just my imagination," Mya whispered. "I realize now that I should've gone away— anywhere for a while after the funeral, but then I had to think about Lily. I'd thought about taking her to Disney World or on a cruise, but I couldn't pull myself out of a funk to make travel arrangements."

"That's because you're still grieving."

"You're probably right."

"I know I'm right," Giles said. "What about now, Mya? Do you still want to get away?"

Easing back, she smiled. "I do if the offer to go to New York before Thanksgiving is still open?"

Giles cradled her face in his hands. "Of course."

"I'm going to ask my neighbor to pick up my mail and keep an eye on the house, and then make and freeze enough food for Lily."

"You don't have to make anything for Lily. I'll call my mother and have her buy the blender."

"Are we going to stay at your place while we're there?"

"No. You and Lily will stay with my parents, because they have a room that's set up as a nursery. Whenever my brother brings his kids over, he doesn't have to lug around a portable crib or playpen."

"How old are your nephews?"

"Three and eighteen months. I'm going to have to watch them around Lily because they are really rough-and-tumble."

"I wouldn't worry too much about our hair-pulling, eye-gouging feisty little girl. I'm sure she'll be able to hold her own against her rough-and-tumble boy cousins."

"No shit!" Giles clapped a hand over his mouth. "Sorry about that."

Mya held out her hand. "Pay up."

"I said I was sorry."

She glared at him. "And I said pay up."

Mya waited for him to reach into a pocket of his jeans and take out a monogrammed money clip. He thumbed through the bills. "My lowest bill is a ten."

"Hand it over because you know you're going to cuss again." She took the bill from his fingers and slipped it into the pocket of her jeans. "Do you cuss at work?"

Giles shook his head. "No. At least not where my assistant can hear me."

"Is it because she's a woman?"

"Yes."

"Is she pretty?"

"I'd say she is. What's up with the inquisition?"

"Just curious."

He angled his head. "Curious about what?" Giles ran a finger down the length of her nose. "You know what they say about curiosity."

"Yeah, I know. It killed the cat."

"And to satisfy your curiosity, gorgeous, there's nothing going on between me and my assistant. I took her with me the last time I flew down to the Bahamas to introduce her to the broker and when I spoke to Kurt the other day, he admitted he's smitten with Jocelyn and plans on stealing her from me."

"What did you say to him about that?"

Giles chuckled. "I told him to go for it because if Jocelyn decides to move to the Bahamas, then I would bypass him and deal directly with her, cutting him out of his commission."

"That's sounds a little cutthroat."

"All gloves are off when someone messes with my employee." Giles told Mya that he had hired and fired a number of assistants until he found everything he wanted and needed in an admin with Jocelyn Lewis. "I'll take you to the office so you can meet her."

"How long do you plan to stay in New York?"

"That's up to you, sweets. I'm electronically connected to my office, so I can be reached anywhere."

"I'd like to be here for Halloween."

"What's up with Halloween?"

"The whole town turns out to celebrate the holiday. There're games, a photo gallery where parents can pose with their children, face-painting for the kids and tailgate parties for the adults. Once the sun sets, there are hayrides and bonfires with people taking turns reading ghost stories. This year, there will also be a costume party in the church basement. The current mayor and town council have continued the tradition of Halloween as a town celebration that began more than twenty years ago to control teens who were vandalizing properties and terrorizing townsfolks."

"If we come back on the thirtieth, then that will give us about five days to hang out in the Big Apple."

Mya's smile was dazzling. "Can you stay here with Lily while I walk across the road to talk to my neighbor?"

Giles kissed her forehead. "Of course."

"I'll begin packing after I come back. I'd planned to go grocery shopping tomorrow, but that can wait until we return."

"Meanwhile I'll call and reserve a flight for tomorrow afternoon."

"Are you certain you'll be able to get a reservation?"

"Quite certain, sweets. We're going to take the company jet."

"Why do you call me that?" Mya asked.

"Sweets?"

"Yes."

Giles winked at her. "That's because you are sweet. Would you prefer I call you darling or my love?"

Mya blushed again. "Sweets will do—for now."

"So are you saying there's the possibility of you becoming my darling or my love?"

"No comment," she said, smiling. Mya returned his wink. "Later, Daddy."

Lines fanned out around Giles's eyes when he smiled. "Later, Mama."

Mya buckled Lily into her car seat on the sleek modern jet before fastening her own. She was on her way to New York with her daughter and the man who, in spite of her busy schedule, intruded into her thoughts during the day *and* at night.

She'd found Giles to be gentle, generous, patient and even-tempered—the complete opposite of the man with whom she had been involved. And if she had had any reservations as to whether he would be a good father, those doubts were quickly dashed when he had become a hands-on father in every sense of the word. Mya wasn't certain whether he was overcompensating because she suspected it hadn't been that way with him and his father.

"Tell me about your family," she said to Giles when he'd turned the white leather seat to face her. Mya wanted to know what to expect before she met the Wainwrights.

He met her eyes. "There's not much to tell. I have an older married brother with two kids and a younger sister. My father heads the legal department for the Wainwright Developers Group, known to insiders as the WDG. Dad, whom everyone calls Pat, is Patrick II and my brother is Patrick III. Patrick works with Dad in the legal department."

"What about your mother and sister?"

"My mother is Amanda. Even though she's lived in New York for forty years, she still talks like a Bostonian. She majored in art history in college and was hired by the Metropolitan Museum as a cataloguer. She put her career on hold after she married and started a family."

"Did she ever go back to the museum?"

"No, but she's still involved in the art world. She works every other weekend at a Second Avenue gallery. My sister Skye just got engaged to her longtime boyfriend a couple of months ago. My mother's freaking out because this summer, Skye gave up her position as a high school guidance counselor to move to Seattle to live with her fiancé."

"A lot of engaged couples live together to save money."

"Skye doesn't have to save money. She has a trust fund."

Mya didn't have to have the IQ of a rocket scientist to know the Wainwrights weren't pleased with Skye's choice in a fiancé. "What does he do?"

Giles frowned. "What doesn't he do? He's had a food truck business that failed. He was in partnership with some of his friends who had a moving business that also went under. Skye claims he's willing to try anything to find his niche. I try not to get involved in her life, but I did tell her his singular calling is getting his hands on her money. Sometimes my sister may let her heart overrule her head, but not her money."

"What did she do?"

"The last time I spoke to her, she said the love of her life was no longer as affectionate as he used to be because she told him she had put herself on a strict budget because she wasn't working."

"It sounds as if lover boy wants her to bankroll his next entrepreneurial venture."

"Bingo! Give that lady a cigar," Giles teased. "It's not nice, but we're all taking bets that she'll be back before the end of the year."

The pilot's voice came through the cabin instructing the crew to prepare the cabin for takeoff. Mya stared out the oval window as the jet taxied down a private runway before it picked up enough speed for a smooth liftoff. All of the furnishings in the aircraft reflected opulence: butter-soft white leather seating for eighteen, teak tables and moldings, flat screen televisions and a fully functional galley kitchen and bathroom.

She glanced over at Lily who'd fallen asleep almost immediately. It was early afternoon and her nap time.

The aircraft climbed, Mya's ears popping with the pressure, and then leveled off to cruising speed.

The five-hundred-mile flight from Charleston to New York on a commercial carrier would take at least four hours, including a connecting flight, and more than eight hours by car, but their flight on the private jet was estimated to take only ninety minutes. They'd decided to forego lunch because Amanda had planned for an early dinner.

Mya's gaze shifted back to Giles, who smiled when their eyes met. His hair was longer than when she first saw him in the lawyer's office. The ends were curling slightly, reminding her of Lily's shiny black waves. Her gaze lingered on his strong mouth. "You promised to tell me why you joined the Marine Corps."

His smile vanished, replaced by an expression of stone. "I did it to spite my mother." Mya wasn't certain if he could hear her audible exhalation. "I'd dated a couple of girls while in college, but none of the relationships were what I'd think of as serious. Meanwhile unbeknownst to me, my mother was colluding with the mother of a young woman who went to high school with me to set us up. A week after graduation, Mom invited the family and some of her friends with kids who'd gone to my high school over for an informal get-together. I'd remembered Miranda as a nice, quiet girl but she wasn't someone I'd date. Everyone was posing with me for the photographer Mom had hired for the event. Two months later, I get a call from one of my cousins that he saw my photograph alongside Miranda's in the engagement section of the *New York Times*."

"Were you two dating?"

"I told you I had no interest in her. When I confronted my mother, she said she'd hoped that Miranda and I would fall in love and eventually marry and she may have also communicated that to Miranda's mother, who'd taken it to the next level. When I demanded they print a retraction, Mom pleaded with me to go along with it for a few months, and then pretend to break it off. What she didn't want to do was embarrass Miranda's family.

"Meanwhile people were calling and congratulating me on my engagement. I tolerated it for a week before walking into a recruitment office and telling the recruiter if he was looking for a few good men, then I was his man. I moved out and checked into a hotel until it was time for me to go to Parris Island, South Carolina for basic training. I'd attained the rank of captain by the time I was deployed to Afghanistan. Meanwhile I hadn't spoken to or communicated with my mother in more than six years. Not knowing whether I'd come back, I called to tell her I was being deployed and I don't remember what she said because she was crying so hard that I lost it. I told her I loved her and then hung up. That's the memory of my mother that continued to haunt me until I returned from my first tour."

Mya hadn't realized she'd bitten her lip until she felt a throbbing pain. "Did you see her when you got back?"

Giles smiled. "Yes. We had a tearful reunion. She claims I'd left a boy and returned a man. I'd put on a lot of muscle and was in peak physical condition. I signed on for a second deployment and after losing several members of my team, I decided to resign my commission. Transitioning to life as a civilian was very difficult for me."

"PTSD?"

He nodded. "It took six months and a kick in the behind from a cousin for me to seek counseling. Once I felt I was in control of my life, I purchased a condo and went to work for WDG."

Reaching over, Mya grasped his hand. "You're one of the lucky ones, Giles. There are a number of veterans from Wickham Falls who've been diagnosed with combat-related post-traumatic stress disorder. More than half the boys who graduated high school with me enlisted in the military because they couldn't find employment now that most of the mines have closed. There was a time when boys graduated or left school to work the mines like their fathers, grandfathers and even great-grandfathers."

Giles threaded his fingers through Mya's. "Do they come back?"

"A few do. Sawyer Middleton and I were in the same graduating class. He enlisted in the army, became a software engineer, made tons of money and then came back last year to head the high school's technology department. He's now married to one of the teachers at the middle school. And there's my neighbor, the deputy sheriff, who also served as a military police officer before coming back to go into law enforcement."

"Now those are what I call success stories." Giles gave her a long, penetrating stare. "You came from Wickham Falls and you did all right."

"That's because my parents were business owners who employed at least two dozen men and women. When it came time for me to go off to college, all my father had to do was write a check. And once I graduated, I didn't have any student debt staring me in the face. I wasn't as lucky as I was blessed that I was adopted into a family that didn't have to count pennies to make ends meet.

"Many of the folks that live in the Falls are the invisible ones that live at or below the poverty line. Twice a year, the church holds a fund-raiser to help families in need. Someone may request a used car so they can get to work, or a single mother with children will ask for monies to fix a leaky roof or repair her hot-water heater. Last Christmas, an anonymous donor gave the church enough toys, clothes and shoes to fill a tractor trailer."

"That's nice."

Her eyebrows lifted a fraction. "That's more than nice, Giles. I'm going to become a donor this year because I intend to purchase at least two hundred children's books for grades one through six."

Giles sat forward. "I'll match your donation."

Her jaw dropped. "Really?"

"Really," he teased. "Let me know what else you want to donate and I'll cover it."

"You don't have to do that."

"Yes, I do if I'm going to live here."

Mya sat back, pulling her hands from his loose grip. "So you've resigned yourself to living in the Falls."

"Do I have a choice if I want to be with my daughter? And becoming an absentee father is not an option."

"No, you don't have a choice," she countered. "It's what Sammie wanted."

Mya watched a hardness settle into Giles's features as he slumped in his chair and glared at her under lowered brows. Mya had stopped questioning her sister's motives where it concerned Lily, but it was apparent Giles hadn't.

She wanted to tell him to suck it up and accept what he couldn't control, otherwise the resentment would fester like an infection. If he could forgive his mother for trying to set him up with a woman he didn't want to marry, then it was time he forgave Sammie and concentrated on making certain his daughter knew she was loved.

Chapter Seven

Giles switched Lily from one arm to the other as he rang the bell to the town house that once was his childhood home. A buzzing sound answered his ring and he shouldered the door open, holding it for Mya to enter the vestibule. The instant he saw the antique table and two straight-backed pull-up chairs, he was reminded that Mya would be the first woman he would bring home to meet his parents. There were a few women that had been his plus-one for various fund-raisers where social decorum dictated he make introductions but nothing beyond that.

"You can leave the bags by the table," he directed the driver who had unloaded their luggage from the trunk of the limo. Reaching into his shirt pocket, he slipped the man a bill.

"Thank you, Mr. Wainwright."

The door closed behind the driver at the same time the one at the opposite end of the hallway opened. Amanda placed both hands over her mouth, walking toward them as if in a trance.

The tears filling her eyes overflowed and ran down the backs of her hands. "Oh my heavens," she whispered through her fingers. She extended her arms. "May I hold her?"

Giles placed Lily in her grandmother's outstretched arms. "She's heavier than she looks."

Amanda's expression spoke volumes. It was obvious she'd instantly fallen in love with her granddaughter. "She's so precious!" She took a step and kissed Giles's cheek. "Thank you for bringing her." She beckoned to Mya. "Come here, darling, and give me a kiss."

Mya approached Giles's mother and pressed her cheek to the older woman's. "Thank you for opening your home to us."

A tender smile parted Amanda's lips. "You are family. So my home is always open to you. Please come in and relax before we sit down to eat. You picked the perfect time to visit New York because we're having an Indian summer and it's warm enough for us to eat in the backyard. Speaking of food," she continued without pausing to take a breath, "Giles told me that you make your own baby food, so I got the blender you need."

"Thank you, Mrs. Wainwright."

Amanda wagged a finger. "None of that Mrs. Wainwright around here. Please call me Mom or Amanda." She wrinkled her delicate nose. "Personally I prefer Mom."

Mya nodded. "Then Mom it is."

Giles rested a hand at Mya's waist. "Go on in, sweets. I'll bring the bags."

He picked up Lily's diaper bag, grasped the handles to Mya's rolling Pullman and followed his mother and Mya down the carpeted hallway to his parents' street-level apartment.

His father purchased the three-story town house when he was still a bachelor. He renovated the entire structure, adding an elevator, and eventually rented the second- and third-story apartments. There had been a time when the entire building was filled with Wainwrights, when the younger Patrick occupied the third floor and Giles the second. They'd joked about moving out without ever leaving home.

He had just walked into the entryway when his father appeared. "Hi, Dad. I didn't expect to see you here."

"When Amanda told me about the baby, I decided anything I didn't finish at the office could wait until another day."

Giles left the Pullman next to a table with an assortment of African- and Asian-inspired paperweights. Pat talking about leaving work on his desk was a practice he should've adopted when his children were younger. Giles had lost count of the number of times his mother waited for her husband to come home and share dinner with the family, until she finally gave up and fed her children before it was time for them to retire for bed.

"So it takes another grandbaby to pull you away from your office."

Pat smiled, the gesture softening his features. Giles had to admit work was probably what had kept his father motivated. At sixty-six, his blond hair had silvered

"FAST FIVE" READER SURVEY

Your participation entitles you to:
✱ **4 Thank-You Gifts Worth Over $20!**

Complete the survey in minutes.

Get **2 FREE Books**

See inside for details.

Dear Reader,

Since you are a lover of our books, your opinions are important to us... and so is your time.

That's why we made sure your **"FAST FIVE" READER SURVEY** can be completed in just a few minutes. Your answers to the five questions will help us remain at the forefront of women's fiction.

And, as a thank-you for participating, we'd like to send you **4 FREE THANK-YOU GIFTS!**

Enjoy your gifts with our appreciation,

Pam Powers

To get your
4 FREE THANK-YOU GIFTS:

✶ Quickly complete the "Fast Five" Reader Survey
and return the insert.

"FAST FIVE" READER SURVEY

1	Do you sometimes read a book a second or third time?	○ Yes ○ No
2	Do you often choose reading over other forms of entertainment such as television?	○ Yes ○ No
3	When you were a child, did someone regularly read aloud to you?	○ Yes ○ No
4	Do you sometimes take a book with you when you travel outside the home?	○ Yes ○ No
5	In addition to books, do you regularly read newspapers and magazines?	○ Yes ○ No

YES! I have completed the above Reader Survey. Please send me my 4 FREE GIFTS (gifts worth over $20 retail). I understand that I am under no obligation to buy anything, as explained on the back of this card.

235/335 HDL GMVN

FIRST NAME	LAST NAME

ADDRESS

APT.#	CITY

STATE/PROV.	ZIP/POSTAL CODE

Offer limited to one per household and not applicable to series that subscriber is currently receiving.
Your Privacy—The Reader Service is committed to protecting your privacy. Our Privacy Policy is available online at www.ReaderService.com or upon request from the Reader Service. We make a portion of our mailing list available to reputable third parties that offer products we believe may interest you. If you prefer that we not exchange your name with third parties, or if you wish to clarify or modify your communication preferences, please visit us at www.ReaderService.com/consumerschoice or write to us at Reader Service Preference Service, P.O. Box 9062, Buffalo, NY 14240-9062. Include your complete name and address.   SE-N17-FFM17

and there were few more lines around his large, intense blue eyes, while spending hours sitting at a desk hadn't taken its toll on his tall, slim physique.

Pat's pale eyebrows lifted. "Something like that. I'd like to talk to you before I officially meet your baby's mother."

Giles went completely still. There was something in the older man's voice he interpreted as censure. "What do you want to talk about?"

"Are you going to marry her?"

"Why would you ask me that?"

"Because Wainwright men don't get women pregnant and not marry them."

Giles struggled to control his temper. At thirty-six, he did not need his father to remind him of how he should live his life. "Have you forgotten that Jordan's father didn't marry his birth mother?" Edward Wainwright, Patrick's cousin, was engaged when he had an affair, an affair that resulted in a child he and his wife secretly adopted and raised as their own.

"I'm not talking about Edward," Pat countered.

"Well, he's the only Wainwright that I can recall who didn't marry his baby mama."

"I'm talking about you, Giles. Your mother tells me you have a child and when I asked if you had or were going to marry the baby's mother, she said no."

"That's because I can't marry her."

"And why the hell not?"

"Because she died, Dad! Mya is not Lily's biological mother. She's her aunt and adoptive mother." Realization suddenly dawned when Giles saw his father's stunned expression. "You thought I'd slept with Mya and got her pregnant?"

"I guess your mother didn't tell me the whole story."

Giles forced a smile. "I guess she didn't." He paused. "Now, are you ready for me to introduce you to my daughter's mother?"

Pat dropped an arm over his son's shoulders. "Lead on."

Giles and his father hadn't always seen eye to eye on a number of things, but rather than go toe to toe with him as his older brother had, Giles would walk away until cooler tempers prevailed. And what he failed to understand was why Patrick would choose to work under their father when the two argued constantly.

They found Mya in the den with Amanda bouncing Lily on her knee. He registered Pat's intake of breath when Mya rose to stand. The action was as graceful and regal as the queen she professed to be.

When Giles had arrived at her house earlier that morning for the ride to the airport, he had been temporarily stunned by her transformation. Missing was the bare face, jeans and T-shirt and socks; they were replaced with a light cover of makeup highlighting her luminous eyes and lush mouth, and a black wool gabardine pantsuit, black-pinstriped silk blouse and matching kitten heels. She had brushed her hair until there was no hint of a curl and pinned it into a chignon on the nape of her neck.

Seeing her like that had jolted him into an awareness that she had been a career woman before giving it up to become a full-time, stay-at-home mother.

Lily was laughing and squealing at the same time. Mya had changed her and given her a bottle during the ride from the airport to Manhattan, and after spending time with his daughter, Giles was now attuned to her moods. She fretted when he didn't feed her fast enough, cried and squirmed when she needed to be changed and loved crawling around on the floor with him. She was much calmer with Mya when she sang or read to her, and whenever they were together in the rocker, it took only minutes for her to fall asleep.

Mya smiled at the tall, slender blond man striding toward her, arms extended. She noticed the only things the older man and Giles shared were height and eye color. A warm glow flowed through her when he hugged her and then kissed her cheek.

"Welcome to the family."

She smiled up at Giles's father. "Thank you, Mr. Wainwright. I'm Mya."

He kissed her other cheek. "Around here, I'm Grandpa." He eased back, his eyes moving slowly over her face. "My granddaughter has a beautiful mother."

Mya wanted to tell him she wasn't Lily's biological mother, but decided to hold her tongue and leave it up to Giles to explain their connection. "Thank you."

"Don't thank me, Mya. Thank the two people who gave you your exquisite looks."

Her smile faded. *I would if I knew who they were,* she thought. "This is Lily, your granddaughter."

Pat stared down at the baby who'd stopped laughing long enough to look up at him. "It's unbelievable." He was unable to disguise the awe in his voice. "She's the spitting image of Skye when she was a baby."

Amanda pressed her mouth to the back of Lily's head. "Speaking of Skye. I called her to tell her about Lily and she says she'll be here tomorrow to meet her niece."

A slight frown appeared between Pat's eyes. "So, that's why she asked me to buy a ticket for her to come home. I thought she'd gotten enough of that leech sucking her dry and had come to her senses and decided to leave him."

"Please, Pat. Let's not talk about that now," Amanda said softly.

Mya was grateful Amanda wanted to change the topic because the last thing she wanted was to become a witness to what had become a source of contention for the Wainwrights. It was never a good thing when parents or family members did not approve of their children's choice in a partner.

A young woman in a gray uniform and white shoes walked into the den. "Mrs. Wainwright. Dinner is ready."

Giles approached Mya and took her hand. "I'll show you where we can wash up."

She waited until they were behind the door of a bathroom off the den, then asked Giles, "Did you tell your father about us?"

He blinked slowly. "He's knows you're not Lily's birth mother, but not much beyond that. He did ask when I was going to marry you, because Wainwright men don't get women pregnant and not marry them."

Mya felt her heart stop and then start up again. "What did you say?"

"I told him that I hadn't gotten you pregnant, so that lets me off the hook about having to marry you."

She exhaled an inaudible sigh. "That's good."

His eyes grew wider. "What's good? Me not having to marry you, or you not wanting to marry me?"

Mya turned on the faucet and then tapped the soap

dispenser. What did he expect her to say? That she could never conceive of marrying him? Or that she would consider marrying him but only if she found herself in love?

"It's not about me marrying you, because I haven't given it a thought one way or the other." She hadn't thought of it because something kept her from completely trusting him. She was certain he loved his daughter, yet she couldn't rid her mind that if he proposed marriage his ulterior motive would be to try and convince her to allow him to share legal custody of Lily.

Giles took a step, pressing his chest to her back. "You wouldn't do it because of Lily?" he whispered in her ear.

Mya closed her eyes as the heat from his body seeped into her hers, bringing with it an awareness of the man who had become so much a part of her day-to-day existence. She woke anticipating his arrival and felt a profound loss whenever he took his leave at the end of the day.

Giles had unexpectedly come into her life, and like the blistering summer heat that did not abate even after the sun had set, everything about him lingered: the firm touch of his mouth on hers when he greeted her, the muscled hardness of his body whenever he leaned into her, the brilliant blue eyes that seemed to know what she was thinking when she'd struggled in vain not to be caught up in the spell of longing whenever she was reminded of how long it had been since a man had made love to her.

There were nights when she woke in a panic from an erotic dream that made her press her face into the pillow to muffle the screams of pleasure as she experienced long-denied orgasms.

"No. There's no way I'm going to allow Lily to become a pawn in a relationship I'd have with any man."

"I'm not any man, Mya. I'm your daughter's father."

She nodded. "I know that. But I'd only marry you if I was in love with you."

Giles pressed a kiss alongside the column of her neck. "So you would consider me as a potential husband."

"Only if I was in love with you," she repeated.

He caressed her waist. "What do I have to do to make you fall in love with me?"

Mya rinsed her hands and then reached for a guest towel from a stack in a ceramic tray. "Just be you," she said cryptically. She dried her hands, dropped the towel in a wastebasket, then turned to see confusion freezing his features. "What's the matter?"

"What do you mean by that?"

She winked at him. "You're a very bright guy. So figure it out."

Giles caught her around the waist. "That's not fair."

"What's not fair?"

"You teasing me."

Mya stared up at him under lowered lashes. "All I'm saying is don't change, Giles. I've gotten to like you a lot. But you flip the script, then it's not going to go so well with us."

Giles's expression hardened. "Please don't compare me to your ex-boyfriend."

"I'm not. Malcolm is who he is, and you are who you are."

"Does this mean I can kiss you? Really kiss you?" he whispered as his head came down.

His mouth covered her before she could form an answer, her lips parting under the tender onslaught that left her shaking from head to toe. This kiss was different from the others because it was as if he was staking his claim. In that instant, she had forgotten all of the men who had ever kissed her as she returned Giles's kiss with a hunger that belied her outward appearance. Her hands came up and cradled his strong jaw as she tried to get even closer.

Then, without warning, it ended. Mya did not want to believe she was cloistered in a bathroom in Giles's parents' home allowing him to kiss her with wild abandon. And she also felt uncomfortable because it was the first time Giles had acted on his lustful stares. Maybe it was because he was more confident in New York being with his family, while she viewed herself as the outsider despite the elder Wainwrights welcoming her with warmth and open arms.

"Please open the door, Giles."

He released her and pushed open the door. "Wait for me."

Mya nodded. She noticed he was breathing as heavily as she, which meant they both were affected by the kiss.

She waited for him to wash and dry his hands, then followed him along a narrow hallway leading to the rear of the house. Mya smothered a gasp when he opened a door to a backyard garden with trees, bushes with late-blooming fall flowers, a man-made waterfall and tiny white string lights entwined with ivy within the framework of a pergola. A table with seating for four was covered with hemstitched linens, crystal stemware, china and brass candelabras. Pat seated Amanda after she placed Lily in a high chair between his chair and his wife's.

Giles pulled out a chair, seating Mya before he claimed his own next to her. "Don't look so worried," he whispered in her ear. "My mother has more than enough experience raising her children and now occasionally babysitting her grandkids."

Mya forced a smile. She wasn't aware her concern for Lily had shown on her face. She realized there would come a time when she would have to let go of her daughter, but knew it wasn't going to be easy.

Amanda smiled across the table. "Mya, I hope you and Giles will let Lily stay with me while you two take some time for yourselves while you're here, and I want to spend as much time with her before you go back to West Virginia."

"Of course," Mya said reluctantly, when Giles nudged her foot with his under the table.

"What about when you go into the gallery?" Pat asked Amanda.

"Not to worry, darling," Amanda crooned. "I'm taking off for as long as Giles and Mya are here. By the way, when are you going back?"

Mya shared a look with Giles. "We plan to stay until at least the thirtieth."

"Bummer," the older woman said between clenched teeth. "I was hoping you'd stay for Halloween because I always take pictures of the kids in their costumes. Last year, both of Patrick's boys were dressed like pumpkins."

"Maybe next year," Giles said, "that is if it's okay with Mya."

Mya nodded. "We'll definitely think about it."

"Is that a promise?" Amanda asked.

"Of course," he replied.

"We'll be back again for Thanksgiving," Mya added.

"What about Christmas?"

Mya smiled. "We'll be here for Christmas."

She was actually looking forward to celebrating Christmas in New York City. It had always been her wish to eat roasted chestnuts from street vendors while strolling along Fifth Avenue to check out the gaily decorated department store windows. She also planned to have Giles take a photo of her and Lily in front of the Christmas tree at Rockefeller Center.

Amanda pressed her palms together. "You have to spend the Christmas week and New Year's with us. Christmas is when the entire family gets together for what becomes somewhat of a never-ending party. The New Year's Eve ball is always a fund-raiser. The family underwrites the cost of the food, drinks and entertainment for folks with deep pockets to donate to the year's designated charity."

Mya sat straight. "Who selects the charity?"

Giles rested a hand over Mya's. "Those who sit on the Wainwright board of directors, who all happen to be family members. This year, they selected the World Vision's water project for Kenya. We've committed to match whatever we raise for the evening."

Suddenly she saw his family in a whole new light. They were using their wealth to help make the world better for those less fortunate.

Mya's attention shifted to several waiters pushing carts with covered dishes onto the patio. She smiled as Lily babbled incessantly while patting the high chair tray. Amanda had asked whether Lily was lactose intolerant because she'd planned to blend macaroni and cheese for the baby. She confided to the child's grandmother that Lily was a joy to feed because the baby wasn't a picky eater.

"Do you eat like this every time you get together?" Mya asked Giles quietly as waiters set out the food. The table was covered with cold and hot dishes ranging from sushi, tuna tartare, daikon and carrot, lobster and crab salads to pasta with a variety of sauces and grilled glazed pork spareribs, Cornish game hens and eggplant.

"Yes." Giles picked up and held the platter of sushi for Mya. "Mom says she likes to be eclectic when it comes to planning a dinner. In other words, a little something for everyone."

"Does your mother cook?"

"Yes. In fact, she's an incredible cook—like her granddaughter's mother." Giles punctuated the compliment when he kissed her hair. "She ordered in tonight because she wanted to get the house ready for us."

His disclosure caught Mya slightly off guard. "I thought you were going to stay in your apartment."

"Not tonight. Tomorrow you can decide what you want to do."

She gave him a sidelong glance. "What's on our agenda?"

He lifted his shoulders. "Not much. I'll probably pop into the office to check in with Jocelyn, and after that, I'm all yours." Giles paused. "Maybe I'll call my cousin Jordan and see if we can stop by and see his new baby."

"I'm going to call my editor and if she has the time, we can share lunch before we go back."

"Are you guys talking about doing something together?" Amanda asked. "Because Pat and I don't mind babysitting if you want to have some alone time."

Mya shook her head. "I...I don't want to impose on—"

"Don't say it," Amanda warned, interrupting her. "It's not as if you asked us to look after her. We're offering. And once Skye gets here I'm willing to bet you won't get to see your daughter again until it's time for you to leave."

Giles draped his free arm over the back of Mya's chair. "Just make certain you don't spoil her so much that she'll be off schedule and not want to sleep at night."

Amanda glared at him. "I did raise three children, so I believe that qualifies me to look after my grandbabies."

Mya rested a hand on Giles's shoulder. "Let it go," she whispered. She didn't want Giles to get into it with his mother about Lily. She planned to give Amanda a detailed schedule for the baby's nap and mealtimes.

"Don't argue with your woman, son, because you'll only lose."

Amanda glared at her husband. "Stay out of their business, Pat."

"I'm not getting into their business, Mandy. I'm just trying to give him some sage advice."

"Advice they probably don't need," Amanda retorted.

Giles picked up a sushi roll with a pair of chopsticks. "Dad's right. I've learned not to get into it with Mya because I usually end up losing."

Mya's eyebrows lifted, questioning. "Usually?" she teased. "You always lose."

Pat grimaced. "Oh-kay," he drawled. "It's time to drop that topic."

Mya agreed when she said, "How often do you dine alfresco?"

"As often as I can," Amanda said. "Once all of the kids were gone, Pat and I talked about selling this place because it's much too big for two people."

"Do you use the entire building?"

"Not anymore. Once Patrick and Giles left, we rented the second- and third-story apartments to doctors, because New York Hospital is within walking distance. But I didn't like being a landlord, so when their leases were up, we decided to use the entire building for out-of-town friends and family. My brother and sisters have thirteen children and at least sixteen grandchildren among them. Whenever they come down from Boston, it's like summer camp with babies underfoot and kids running up and down the stairs."

Giles smiled. "Don't let Mom fool you. She loves it when the house is filled to capacity."

Amanda nodded. "He's right. When Pat and I were first married, we'd planned on having six children."

"What made you change your mind?" Giles asked his mother.

"I didn't realize how much work went into child rearing. I grew up with a nanny, so I never saw my mother frazzled or overwhelmed. And because I missed that close contact with her, I decided early on that I'd be a hands-on mother. I had your brother and you came along eighteen months later, and now when I look back, I know I was experiencing some postpartum depression. That's when I decided to wait at least five years before getting pregnant again. I felt my family was complete because I had my sons and a daughter."

"And now we have two grandsons and a grand-daughter," Pat said in a low, composed voice.

Mya managed to conceal a smile when she pretended interest in the food on her plate as Amanda recalled some of the tricks her sons had played on her. They would hide in one of the many closets in the town house and wait for her to search the entire building to find them.

Amanda wiped away traces of mac and cheese from Lily's chubby cheeks. "I was almost at my wit's end when I decided to turn the tables on them. One day when they left for school, I had a workman come in and change the doorknobs on all of the closets. When they realized they needed a key to open them, it put an end to their disappearing acts. So if Lily is anything like her father, then she's going to be quite a challenge."

Mya nodded. "Thanks for the advance warning."

"I wasn't that bad," Giles said, in defense of himself.

"Not bad, just mischievous," Amanda countered. "Even though I love being a mother, it still doesn't compare to being a grandmother. You'll see, Mya, once Lily's married and has children."

"That's not going to be for a while," Mya said.

"That's where you're wrong because they grow up so fast that you'll wonder where the time went. I preach that to my son Patrick and thankfully he's taken my advice and spends a lot of his free time with his boys."

"That's something I didn't do with my kids," Pat admitted. He met Mya's eyes. "I let work consume me and by the time I left the office, my children were in bed. It was the same in the morning. I was up and out before they sat down to breakfast. I know I can't make it up with my children, but I promised Mandy that it's going to be different with the grandkids."

I have to learn that being a father is a lot more than offering financial support. Now Mya knew what Giles meant. Although his father had financially supported his family, it was the emotional support he had withheld.

"None of us grow up knowing how to parent," Mya said in a quiet voice. "We learn on the job. I've read a lot of books on child rearing, and there's no definitive blueprint for becoming the perfect mom or dad. Lily has her own little personality and there may come a time when we're going to be at odds with each other and I'm going to have to accept that. It's different with girls than boys because of hormones. Once we were teenagers, my sister and I weren't very nice to our mother or each other, but that didn't mean we didn't love one another. My mother admitted she went through the same thing with her own mother, so she waited for us to come to our senses."

Giles set down his fork. "Even though I'm a newbie when it comes to being a parent, I have no doubt Mya is going to make me a better father."

"Don't be a fool and let her get away from you," Pat said to his son.

"Patrick!" Amanda admonished. "Why are you interfering?"

"I am not interfering. I'm just stating a fact." Pat pointed at Giles. "If you let Mya get away—"

"Enough, Dad," Giles said, cutting him off. "Mya and I will be together for a long time."

"How long is long?" Pat questioned.

"Patrick Harrison Wainwright!" Amanda said, her voice rising in annoyance. "Mind your business!"

"Stop it, Dad. Mya and I want the best for Lily, and we will do everything within our power to make certain she knows she's loved and protected."

Mya felt like an interloper when she felt tension in Giles as he engaged in a stare down with his father. She wondered if the older Wainwright felt his son had been irresponsible when he'd gotten a woman pregnant, or resentful that Lily wasn't a Wainwright.

Pat's comments cast a pall over the remainder of dinner as everyone, except Lily, appeared interested in eating what was on their plates rather than engage in further conversation. Mya was certain everyone was relieved when the table was cleared and no one opted for coffee and dessert.

Giles pushed back his chair. "I'm going for a walk. Do you want to come with me?"

Mya turned to look at Giles. "What about Lily?"

"She's going to be all right, sweets. Remember my mother raised three kids, so she's certified to take care of an eight-month-old."

I'm going to have to learn to let go and not become a helicopter mom, Mya thought. The last thing she wanted to become was overbearing and smothering where her daughter's love would turn into resentment.

"Okay. Can you wait for me to go inside and change?"

Giles assisted her up. "Of course."

Chapter Eight

Giles experienced the peace that had evaded him for years as he held Mya's hand when they strolled along Second Avenue. She had changed into a pair of jeans, pullover sweater and running shoes.

"I'm sorry about my father," he said after a comfortable silence.

"Don't apologize, Giles. Your father said what he wanted."

He glanced at her delicate profile. "And what's that?"

"He wants us together and I'm willing to bet that he also wants Lily to become a Wainwright."

"You're probably right about his granddaughter becoming a Wainwright. Dad views being a Wainwright as akin to American royalty. My great-grandfather came to this country broke as a convict. Like so many other immigrants during the turn of the century, he and his new bride shared a railroad flat on the Lower East Side with several other families. Patrick took odd jobs, while my great-grandmother took in wash to pay their share of the rent. Patrick managed to get a position as a building superintendent for several buildings on Houston Street, which allowed him to move into an apartment rent-free. Meanwhile his wife had become quite an accomplished seamstress and would occasionally sew for people in show business. They had three sons and a daughter, who died from diphtheria before her fifth birthday.

"James and Harrison knew their only path out of poverty was education. They graduated high school and enrolled in City College for a tuition-free college education. James became a teacher, while Harrison went into law. Meanwhile, Wyatt, the middle son took the opposite path of his brothers. He dropped out of school in the tenth grade and hired himself out as a bagman for a local thug running an illegal numbers operation. The police never suspected Wyatt because he looked much younger than sixteen. He made certain to stay off the streets during school hours to evade the truant officers, and after a while, he made more in a week than his law-abiding siblings because he had a gift for playing and hitting the numbers. His father gave him an ultimatum—go back to school and get a high school diploma or move out."

"Did he move out or go back to school?"

"Yes. He went back to school. I'm telling you this because I want you to know that the Wainwrights haven't always been legit."

Mya leaned into him. "Don't forget so-called robber barons used dubious means to become very wealthy men."

Giles told Mya that his great-uncle had amassed a

small fortune and, with the assistance of his gangster mentor, bought a run-down tenement and renovated it. He moved into one of the apartments and rented the others to his criminal friends who used them for everything from bookmaking to fencing stolen goods. However, Wyatt drew the line when it came to drugs and prostitution. He was sweet on a young black girl who lived in the neighborhood but nothing came of it because interracial relationships were taboo at the time.

"Once he bought his second building, Wyatt decided it was time to leave his criminal past behind. He got one of his criminal cronies to buy him out and he hired Harrison to set up a corporation for his real estate business. Wyatt had become quite adept at buying abandoned properties, renovating them and selling them at a huge profit. He was flipping properties decades before it became popular. After he'd amassed enough money, he decided to build instead of renovate. He'd become the successful Wainwright son while the other two had to depend on others for their salaries. Wyatt made peace with his father and invited his brothers to join him when he set up the Wainwright Developers Group. Wyatt had yet to celebrate his fortieth birthday when he became a real estate mogul and a multimillionaire. Although he's semi-retired, Wyatt hasn't come that far from the streetwise, baby-faced gangster to family patriarch. He still has a gun in his desk drawer.

"There are times when my father forgets where the Wainwrights came from because he grew up privileged. We all attended private schools, traveled abroad during school holidays and were expected to marry women with impeccable pedigrees. That was okay for my parents and their siblings, but my generation has,

as you say, flipped the script because we marry whoever the hell we want."

Mya giggled softly. "Y'all have gone rogue."

Giles gave her fingers a gentle squeeze. "It feels
good to throw off the shackles of a tradition that money
must marry money."

There came another period of silence before Mya
spoke again. "Is your father upset that Lily is not a
Wainwright?"

"That's only part of it. My father may not have been
there for many of the milestones in our childhood but
there was something he relentlessly preached to me
and my brother and that was making certain not to get
a woman pregnant if we had no intention of marrying
her. He said never to rely on a woman to prevent contra-
ception because there was no way of knowing whether
she was taking an oral conceptive or had an IUD. He
said that the one thing we could be certain of was using
our own condoms. His suspicions came from several
of his college buddies who became fathers before they
were ready when their girlfriends claimed they were
on the pill, or they'd used the girl's condoms."

"Do you resent becoming a father before you were
ready?"

Giles stopped in the middle of the sidewalk and
cradled Mya's face between his palms. "No. I never
would've met you if she hadn't been born."

Her hands circled his strong wrists. "This is not
about me."

"Isn't it, sweets? It's all about you *and* Lily. You two
are a package deal. I can't have one without the other."

Mya's eyes narrowed. "What do you want, Giles?"

He smiled and attractive lines fanned around his eyes. "I want you and I want Lily in my life."

"We are in your life," she argued softly. "Didn't you say we're a family?"

"Yes, but not in the legal sense. I want you to marry me."

A nervous laugh escaped Mya. "You want me to marry you so you'll have some legal claim on me and my daughter."

"Wrong, Mya. I want to marry you because you're the missing piece in my life. I'm no choirboy when it comes to women. I've slept with women I liked and some I didn't like because I needed a physical release, and I'm not very proud of that. Whenever I'm around you, I feel something I've never felt with any other woman and please don't tell me it's because of Lily because right now she doesn't figure into the equation.

"When I went into combat, I didn't know that if I survived whether I'd ever be the same. I did survive but lived in my own personal hell and was racked with guilt because I did survive when other men under my command didn't. Facing death forced me to acknowledge my own mortality and to live each day as if it was my last. I've never been in love with a woman, but if what I'm beginning to feel for you is love, then dammit, I'm willing to embrace it."

Going on tiptoe, Mya brushed a light kiss over his mouth. "Why don't we take it slow and see where it leads."

"Is that a yes?"

She shook her head. "It's not a yes but a maybe. And because I'm an old-fashioned Southern girl, then

I expect you to court me before you ask for my hand in marriage."

Giles flashed a smile, exhibiting a mouth filled with perfectly aligned white teeth. "How long do I have to court you, Miss Mountain State Queen?"

"At least six months of courtship."

He quickly did the calculations in his head. "We met for the first time in September, so next February or March seems appropriate for us to announce our engagement."

"You can't talk about an engagement when I haven't said whether I'll marry you."

"Will you at least consider marrying me?"

Mya paused before giving Giles an answer. She knew she was falling for him—hard—and she had sought to test Giles to uncover whether he wanted her as a wife because he loved her and not because she was Lily's mother. She couldn't dismiss the nagging suspicion that she had become the conduit through which he would eventually claim his daughter legally.

She nodded. "Right now I can say truthfully that I will consider it. And if I say yes, then I don't want a short engagement."

"How long do you want the engagement to be?"

"At least a year." Dating for six months and marrying a year later would allow Mya more than enough time to know if she could trust Giles completely.

"That means we'll marry sometime the following spring."

She nodded. "Do you expect me to sign a prenuptial agreement?"

Giles released her face as his hands curled into tight fists. "Hell no! What made you ask that?"

She withdrew from him without moving when she saw rage lurking in the blue orbs and the skin drawn tight over his cheekbones. "Just checking. I don't want you to think I'm marrying you for your money."

"And I don't want you to think I want to marry you because of Lily."

Mya slipped her arm through his. "Now that we've settled that, we don't have to bring it up again."

She knew Giles was still bothered by her query because a muscle flicked angrily at his jaw. He was probably so used to women falling all over themselves to get his attention because of his name, looks and money that no doubt he believed she was no exception. And no matter how much she liked him, Mya wasn't going to allow her heart to rule her head.

There was a time when she disliked him intensely when they first met, but that was then. Now she enjoyed his company. And she never tired of watching him interact with Lily. At first, she'd believed he was drawn to the little girl because of vanity—that Lily reminded him of his sister—but after a while Mya knew his affection for the child was genuine. He had assumed the responsibility of reading to her before putting her in the crib for her nap. The few times Mya had looked in on them, she found Lily curled up on his chest asleep while he cradled her in his large hands. She had wanted to chastise him for holding her but held her tongue when she backed out of the room. That was when she had to remind herself he shared DNA with the baby and she didn't. That a judge had ruled that she was legally

Lily's mother, while Giles would have to navigate the legal system to claim his daughter.

They continued walking and stopped in front of a sports bar where the doors were open and patrons were yelling at the top of their lungs. "I used to hang out here whenever I came home from college," Giles said.

She noticed his eyes were fixed on one of the many screens. "Do you want to go in?" He looked at her, seemingly shocked by her suggestion.

"You don't mind?"

Mya tugged at his arm. "Of course not. After a few beers, I'll probably scream with the others."

"I didn't know you liked baseball."

"I got into it when I lived in Chicago."

"White Sox or Cubs?"

Her smile was dazzling. "Cubbies, of course."

Giles managed to shoulder his way inside, pulling her behind through the crowd standing three deep at the bar. He managed to find a table for two in a corner near the kitchen and signaled the waiter for two beers.

"Is it always crowded like this?" she shouted to be heard over the babble of voices.

"Yes. But there's more people than usual because it's the first game of the World Series."

Even though she wasn't an avid sports fan, Mya enjoyed the camaraderie of getting together with friends and colleagues to watch an occasional game. And cheering for a particular team allowed her to get swept up in the excitement going on around her.

She had asked Giles to give her time to consider his proposal because she was still grieving the loss of her sister. And it would also take time to accept the reality that she would eventually sleep with the same man as her niece's mother.

After the second beer, she found herself caught up in the hysteria that swept through the sports bar like a lighted fuse. She watched Giles when he recognized someone from his past. There were a lot of rough hugs and back slaps before he introduced her as his girlfriend.

It was close to ten when they returned to the house, and Mya discovered she was slightly tipsy from downing two beers. "I'm under the influence," she whispered to Giles as he unlocked the front door.

"From two beers?"

"Yes."

"Either you are a cheap drunk or you don't get out enough."

Her lips parted in a lopsided grin. "Both," she slurred.

"Why don't you go upstairs and turn in while I check on Lily?"

"We'll check together." There wasn't a day since Sammie came home with the baby that Mya hadn't checked on Lily before turning in for the night.

They found Amanda and Pat sitting together in the den watching an all-news channel. Pat had his arm around his wife while she rested her head on his shoulder. Despite Amanda having to raise her children alone even though she had a husband, she had stayed with him. Was it because, Mya mused, she did not believe in divorce? Or did she fear not having a man in her life? Or was it because she loved him and accepted his shortcomings?

Giles placed a finger over his mouth when he led her in the direction of the nursery.

The nursery was set up in an alcove off the master bedroom where Pat or Amanda had easy access in the event one of their grandchildren required their immediate attention. Lily was sleeping soundly on her back in one of the two cribs. Her tiny rosebud mouth twitched as if she wanted to smile at something that had amused her. Mya's loving gaze lingered on the long dark lashes resting on rosy pink cheeks and the coal-black hair grazing her rounded forehead.

She leaned against Giles's body when he put an arm around her waist. Turning her head, she kissed his neck below his ear at the same time his fingers tightened against her ribs. They stood watching the sleeping child, and then as if on cue, they walked out of the room.

"Baby's in bed, and now it's time for Mama to turn in before she falls on her face," he said softly.

Mya giggled. "I told you that I'm not much of a drinker."

Bending slightly, Giles scooped her up in his arms. "You didn't lie about that."

She buried her face against the column of his strong neck. "I never lie." Giles carried her up the back staircase and into the second-floor bedroom Amanda had assigned her. He placed her on the bed and lay beside her.

"Do you need help getting undressed?"

Mya gave him a crooked smile. "I don't think so. I'm just going to lie here for a few minutes, and then I'm going to get up and take a shower."

Giles shifted until they lay facing each other. "What

if I hang around to make certain you don't slip in the bathroom?"

"Sorry, handsome, but no thanks. If you think you're going to get a peek at my goodies before it's time, then you're deluding yourself."

Giles flashed an irresistibly devastating grin. "Please don't tell me you're going to make me wait until our wedding night before I can sneak a peek."

"Yes."

He affected a frown. "That's cruel and unusual punishment."

"No, it's not. Remember what I told you about courting me."

"What about a sniff?"

Before Mya could reply, Giles sprang up, shifted her effortlessly until she lay on her back and planted his face between her thighs. "No!" she screamed before laughing hysterically. She laughed even harder when he made growling noises like rutting bull.

"Don't make another sound," he warned, grinning, "or my folks will think something happened to you."

Mya waited for him to inch his way up her body, while supporting his weight on his forearms. Her body shook as her laughter turned to giggles. "You're incorrigible."

Giles kissed her chin. "No, I'm not. It's just when I see something I want, I go all in."

She sobered and met his eyes. Mya knew she had to stop denying what she so obviously wanted and needed. She'd told Giles that she wanted to wait for their wedding night to make love, yet knew realistically she didn't want to wait that long. "I've changed my mind," she said in a quiet voice. "I'm not going to make you wait until we're married for us to make love. It's just that I don't want our relationship to be based on sex like yours and Sammie's."

"That's the only thing we shared because she didn't want anything else."

"Don't forget Lily," Mya reminded him. She gave him a long, penetrating stare. "You don't like it, do you, when I mention Sammie's name?"

"Why would you say that?"

"Because you get a little frown between your eyes whenever I talk about her."

"I didn't realize that," he admitted. "Maybe it's because whenever you mention her name, I'm reminded that she was your sister."

Mya nodded. "But I am *not* my sister. Sammie was complex and almost impossible to figure out but I'd learned to accept and love her in spite of her peculiar idiosyncrasies."

"It would be a sad world if we all looked alike and thought alike."

"You're so right, love. Now let me get up so I can get ready for bed."

"Where's my night-night kiss?"

Her lips found their way to his, shivering slightly as the contact sent currents of desire racing through her. Giles returned the kiss, increasing the pressure until her lips parted; his tongue searched the recesses of her mouth until she moaned as if in pain. Her tongue touched and dueled with his and ignited a fire that threatened to consume her mind and body.

"Giles," she moaned, the sound coming from somewhere she didn't know existed.

"I know, baby," he whispered against her trembling

lips. He rolled off her body and stood at the side of the bed, staring at her heaving breasts. "Good night, my sweet."

Mya stared up at the ceiling and heard rather than saw him leave the bedroom as he closed the door behind him. Groaning, she turned over on her belly and pounded the mattress. Giles had only kissed her and now she was like a cat in heat. She had changed her mind about them making love because she knew she could not hold off not allowing Giles to make love to her until they were engaged, because she wanted him to want her for herself as if he'd never met Sammie or fathered Lily.

And it wasn't for the first time that she blamed herself for not having as much as experience with the opposite sex as her sister. She'd dated a few boys in high school, but none reached the point where they were intimate. It was in her second year in college that she had her first serious relationship with an adjunct lecturer from a nearby college. He was older, divorced and responsible for awakening her dormant sexuality. They slept together for two years until he secured another position out of the state. It was another three years before she dated again. But it lasted less than four months before she called it quits.

After she returned to Wickham Falls and was appointed to teach at the college, she finally accepted Malcom Tate's invitation to have dinner with him. She had been reluctant because they worked together. She enjoyed his company because he was closer to her age and they had a lot in common. The exception was temperament. She was composed while he was volatile and that did not bode well for a future together.

Mya closed her eyes and willed her mind blank. So much had happened in the past year that she needed a daily journal to record the events: she'd become an aunt, buried her sister and become a mother, and now she had committed to share her life and future with her daughter's father. The million-dollar question was: what's next? She wasn't in love with Giles but with time she knew she would come to love him.

She opened her eyes and slipped off the bed. She had to get up and shower before falling asleep in her clothes.

Mya woke the same time as she did every morning. Her internal clock indicated it was time for her to get up. She completed her ablution in record time because she wanted to be up and dressed before Lily woke.

She made her way down the staircase to the wing of the house with the master bedroom. The door was closed. When Giles mentioned that his parents had installed a nursery in their home, she did not think it would be within their bedroom. Mya knew she would have to wait to see Lily.

Her sock-covered feet were silent on the gleaming parquet floor when she walked down a wide hallway and peered into exquisitely furnished rooms. Paintings, wall hangings and fragile vases validated Giles's claim that his mother had earned a degree in art history. The spaces were reminiscent of rooms in museums with priceless objets d'art. She lingered outside one room with tables and curio cabinets filled with obelisks and sculptures and carvings of Egyptian cats, jackals and crocodiles. She walked down a hallway with framed prints of impressionists, cubists and modern artists and turned into a large gourmet kitchen.

Mya swallowed a gasp of surprise when she saw Pat and Giles sitting together in a breakfast nook. She did not know why, but she hadn't expected them to be up so early. It was only 5:45 a.m. Giles wore a white T-shirt and jeans, while his father was dressed for work. She could not pull her eyes away from Giles's muscular upper body. His clothes had concealed a man in his prime and in peak conditioning.

"Good morning," Mya said cheerfully.

Giles jumped up. Apparently she had startled him. "Good morning." He approached her as she entered the kitchen. He cupped the back of her head and brushed a kiss over her parted lips.

Easing back, she nodded to Pat. "Good morning, Grandpa."

Pat lifted his cup of coffee in acknowledgment. "Good morning. You're quite the early bird."

"I get up early to take care of Lily."

"You don't have to do that with Mandy hovering over her like a mother hen." He patted the bench seat next to him. "Come sit down. Giles, please make her a cup of coffee. I was talking to Giles about Mandy and I taking Lily to the Bronx Zoo today, and he said I'd have to ask you. I plan to go into the office this morning for a couple of hours, then come back and pick up Mandy and the baby. We keep a stroller, car seat and a baby carrier on hand, so transporting her shouldn't be a problem. Mandy says she's going to make her food and store it in a bag that will keep it warm, along with bottles of milk and water."

"If you want my permission, then you have it." Taking Lily to the zoo was a way for them to bond with her. "What do you have planned for tomorrow?"

Pat flashed a sheepish grin. "We were talking about possibly driving up to Boston to introduce Lily to Mandy's brother and sisters. I have a feeling she wants to show her off," he said under his breath. "Skye's scheduled to arrive today, so we'll wait and see if she wants to come with us."

"If you go to Boston, Dad, then that's not going to be a day trip," Giles said as he walked to the breakfast nook carrying a mug of steaming hot coffee. He set the mug on the table. "Coffee with a splash of milk and one sugar for the pretty lady."

"That's what I told your mother. But she says if we hire a driver, then we can do it in a day."

Mya stared at the liquid in the mug. Lily had become somewhat of a novelty to the Wainwrights and she realized they wanted to spend as much time with her before she went back to Wickham Falls. She ignored the anxiety tightening the muscles in her stomach when she thought of not seeing her baby for more than twenty-four hours.

"You can keep her overnight if you want."

Pat's face lit up like the rays of the rising sun. "Bless you, my child."

Giles sat down next to Mya and combed his fingers through her unbound hair. "What do you want to do today?"

She shivered slightly from his light touch when his finger traced the outline of her ear. "Other than a little shopping, I'm open to whatever you want."

"I'd like to take you into the office to meet Jocelyn. After that, you can shop until you drop."

"Who's shopping?" Amanda asked. Bending slightly, she placed Lily on the floor and the little girl crawled over to Mya.

"I am." Mya scooped Lily off the floor. Amanda had given Lily a bath, combed her hair and secured a lock of hair atop her head with a narrow white ribbon. "Good morning. Your grandma made you look so pretty with that ribbon in your hair."

Amanda smiled. "You don't know how long I've waited to put a ribbon in a little girl's hair."

Giles stood up and kissed his mother. "Something tells me you're partial to girls."

Pinpoints of color suffused her fair complexion. "That's not true. I love my sons as much as I love my daughter, but it's different when it comes to dressing little girls."

Giles kissed her again. "Just teasing. Do you want coffee?"

"Yes, please." Amanda sat down next to her husband. "Do you want to eat breakfast here or do you plan to grab something at the office?"

"If it won't be any trouble, I'd like to eat here."

Amanda patted the shoulder of his crisp white shirt. "Of course it's not any trouble."

Mya waited until Giles brought his mother's coffee before handing off Lily to him. "I'm going to help your mother fix breakfast."

Amanda appeared surprised by her offer when she said, "You really don't have to help me."

"But I want to. I'm not used to sitting around doing absolutely nothing."

"That's because you don't know how to relax," Giles interjected.

"That's because mothers aren't allowed to relax," Amanda countered. She took a sip of coffee and stared at Mya over the rim. "Because you've pierced Lily's ears, I have a set of earrings I'd like to give you for her. And once she turns sixteen, she'll inherit the pearls and matching earrings my grandmother gave me for my sixteenth birthday."

Mya was slightly taken aback with the generous offer. She'd noticed the magnificent strand of South Sea pearls and matching studs Amanda wore the night before. "Don't you want to give the pearls to your daughter?"

Amanda slowly shook her head. "There's a little wicked tale attached to the baubles. My grandfather died suddenly, leaving my young and attractive grandmother a very eligible widow. After a respectable period of mourning, men came calling on her. She went out with some and rejected a number of others. What she suspected was that most were after her money. So she decided to test them. In other words, put your money where your mouth is. She told each of them that her birthday was coming up and she wanted jewelry as a gift. Some gave her earrings and others broaches. There was one gentleman in particular who'd asked her father what was her favorite jewel. He told him pearls. And not the ordinary cultured pearls but the golden South Sea variety.

"The potential suitor paid someone to sail to Tahiti and bring him back enough thirteen millimeter pearls for a necklace and earrings. It took nearly four months but when he presented my grandmother with the pearls, she decided he was the one. They were married a year later and she gave him six children—all boys. I was her only granddaughter, so I inherited all of her jewelry. I've put aside some for Skye, and the rest I was saving for my granddaughter."

Mya knew Amanda loved talking about her family and there was no doubt she had many, many more stories to tell. "Lily's a very lucky little girl."

"After breakfast, we'll go through the jewelry and you can pick out what else you want for Lily."

Pat cleared his throat. "I hope you save some for Patrick because he and Bethany may change their minds and have another baby. And it could be a girl."

Amanda shook her head. "That's not happening because Bethany told me she's done having children. I didn't press her about it, so I'm assuming she's either having or had a procedure so she wouldn't get pregnant again."

Sitting in the kitchen and talking was something Mya missed with her family. Her father would come home and vent about his workmen or customers who changed their minds after he'd designed a table or a headboard. Then it was her mother who updated everyone with news from home about a relative who'd been caught cheating on his wife or a wife cheating on her husband. Mya never thought of it as malicious gossip but idle chatter because there wasn't anything else to talk about. Occasionally they would discuss politics and the fact the country was going to hell in a handbasket as it had over the past two hundred years. What Graham and Veronica sought to do was shield their daughters from local gossip, but as they got older what they heard from their classmates they never repeated to their parents. Their peers whispered about girls who'd slept with every boy on the football team, and several underage girls who'd sought to hide their relationships with older men, and then there were the boys and girls who were gay—rather than come out they waited until graduation to leave Wickham Falls to escape the taunts and harassment to live openly with a same-sex partner.

And nothing had changed when Sammie came back to the Falls to live and people began noticing that she was putting on weight. Once her condition was evident, folks wanted to know who the father was. Both she and Sammie were mute because her sister wasn't the first single mother in Wickham Falls and she definitely would not be the last.

Mya joined Amanda at the cooking island as they selected the items needed to make breakfast for their men.

Chapter Nine

Mya stared at the emerald-cut ruby ring surrounded by a double halo of flawless blue-white diamonds set in twenty-four carat gold on her left hand. Amanda had insisted she wear it because the blood-red stone was the perfect match for her golden skin tones.

"I can't take it."

"You can and you will," Amanda insisted. "That ring belonged to my mother but she hardly ever wore it because she didn't like red. And the gold made her pale skin look washed-out."

"It's magnificent."

Amanda smiled. "I agree." She pressed her palms together. "Now let's see what else is in this so-called treasure trove I can give away."

Mya was in awe when Amanda handed her a pair of diamond earrings for Lily. They totaled a carat, set in platinum and the accompanying appraisal certified they were flawless.

"I think Lily and I are good for now," she said when Amanda selected a diamond bracelet. "Why don't you wait until she's older when she can really appreciate the sentimentality. Then she can say Grandma gave me this ring for my tenth birthday or this necklace for my high school graduation."

Amanda nodded. "You're right."

Mya hugged the older woman. "I'll always remember today because of the ring."

"So will I, because it is the day I got my second daughter." She pulled back. "I get on Pat about interfering in his kids business only because I don't want him to make the same mistake I did when I tried matching Giles up with my best friend's daughter. He punished me in the most severe way possible when he disappeared for years. No one in the family knew where he was, and there was a point when I didn't know whether he was dead or alive. I had no idea he'd joined the military until he called to let me know he was being deployed. It was that day I swore I would never meddle in my children's lives again. Pat and I are not happy with the man Skye has chosen to live with, but I refused to say anything to her. When she's had enough, she'll leave him. There is one thing I know about the Wainwrights. They are survivors."

Amanda was right. Sammie had died so that Lily would survive. And not only was Lily a survivor but Mya knew she was also a survivor. She watched Amanda lock the box and return it to a wall safe behind a framed Rembrandt reproduction.

"Art students would love your home."

"You're probably right. I had a photographer approach me with an offer to photograph the house for a slick architectural magazine but I turned him down. Some of the pieces are originals and many are copies, and I don't want to invite thieves who use the most devious ways to break into someone's property. It was only after I became an empty nester that I decided to turn the house into somewhat of a museum. Whenever the grandkids come over, I simply close the doors to the rooms with the art. I've catalogued and have every piece appraised, and I've indicated in my will who gets what. I will not have my children fighting one another over material items."

Mya wanted to tell Lily's grandmother that she and Sammie hadn't had that problem. Their parents had divided everything they owned evenly. Amanda was candid when she said there had been a time when she'd had a live-in housekeeper, but now she valued her privacy, and the housekeeper only came in two days a week and whenever she hosted a get-together.

Mya nearly doubled over in laughter when she saw Lily crawling along the carpeted hallway to get away from Giles, who was on all fours crawling after her. Piercing screams rent the air as Giles pounced on Lily and pretended to gobble her up. Pressing her back against the wall, Mya moved past them and took the staircase to her bedroom.

Mya emerged from the en suite bath after brushing her teeth to find Giles sitting on a chair bouncing Lily on his knees. "You better be careful juggling her like that before she barfs on you."

Giles lifted several strands from Lily's moist forehead. "That's all right. My princess can do anything she wants." He glanced up, his gaze lingering on her hand. "Where did you get that ring?"

She held out her hand, fingers outstretched. "Your mother gave it to me. She said it belonged to your grandmother."

Giles dropped a kiss on the back of her hand. "It's beautiful."

"I agree."

"She also gave me a pair of diamond earrings for Lily, but she won't be able to wear them until she's older."

"Mom loves giving gifts. You'll discover that when we come back for Christmas."

Mya knelt near the chair, her eyes meeting Giles's. "Are you going to miss not living in New York?"

Giles pressed his forehead to Mya's. "What I'd miss is not being with you and Lily. I could live anywhere as long as we're together. Dad and I had a very candid talk earlier this morning about what it means to be a father. His father was a workaholic and Dad followed in his footsteps. I hadn't realized how much I resented my father not being around for dinner until I shared this morning's breakfast with you and Lily. Night after night, I'd watch my mother hold back tears when she stared at the empty chair at the opposite end of the table waiting for my father because he was always running very late. One night, Patrick had had enough when he raised his voice to Mom and told her that she was deluding herself if she expected her husband to share dinner with his family. That must have been a wake-up call for her because she never waited for him again."

"Lily and I will not eat with you whenever you leave on business."

"Not if you travel with me. I'd like you to apply for a passport for Lily, so when we fly down to the Bahamas, she can come with us."

Mya stared at him, momentarily shocked with his offer of wanting her to accompany him on a business trip. However, a silent voice nagged at her that he'd offered because he didn't want to be away from Lily. If not, then he could've suggested they leave the baby with his parents until their return.

"How long do you normally stay?" she asked when she recovered her voice.

"It can be two days to more than a week. Meanwhile, you and Lily can have the run of the resort."

"Does it belong to WDG?"

Giles rubbed their noses together. "Yes. You're now unofficially a Wainwright because you just called Wainwright Developers Group WDG."

She smiled. "That's because I've heard you refer to the company as WDG, and it's also stamped on the sides of the jet."

"You don't miss much, do you?"

"Nope."

Giles glanced at his watch. "I'm going to my place to get dressed, and when I come back, we'll leave to go shopping"

"Do you live far from here?"

"No. I'm about twenty blocks away and closer to the river. I'll take you there before we come back tonight."

"When is your sister coming in?"

"Her flight is scheduled to touch down around one this afternoon. Dad has already arranged for a car to pick her up. She'll be jet-lagged for a few days, then watch out. If you think Lily's a squealer, then you have to hear Skye. It's ear-shattering."

Mya extended her arms. "Give me the little squealer. I'll be dressed and ready by the time you come back."

Mya stood in the private elevator with Giles as the car rose swiftly to where WDG occupied the entire top floor in the Third Avenue office building. Giles had informed her that although WDG owned the building, the company leased office space to other businesses on the other twenty-six floors, and space on every floor of the high-rise structure was filled to capacity.

His attire harked back to the time when she'd first encountered him in Preston McAvoy's conference room. The dark gray suit, white dress shirt, royal blue silk tie and black wingtips reminded her he was a businessman who bought and sold multimillion-dollar properties with the stroke of a pen. She eschewed entertaining negative thoughts, yet she couldn't rid her head of the fact that Giles would become disenchanted living in Wickham Falls, that if they married he would somehow concoct a scheme where they would have to live in New York.

"You look very nice."

Mya inclined her head. "Thank you."

She had packed several outfits she had deemed business attire. When many instructors and professors favored jeans and running shoes, she had opted for pantsuits and conservative dresses. Today, she had selected a black lightweight wool sheath dress with a matching hip-length jacket. Sheer black nylons and a pair of leather-and-suede booties were in keeping with the favored ubiquitous New York City black. The elevator opened to doors with the company's name etched in silver across the glass.

Resting his hand at the small of Mya's back, Giles swiped a key card and when the light changed from red to green, he pushed it open. The receptionist sitting behind a mahogany counter smiled at him. The screen on the wall behind her displayed the time, temperatures and headlines of countries from around the world.

"Welcome back, Giles."

He returned her smile. "Thank you, Linda." Giles escorted Mya up three stairs to an expansive space covered in pale gray carpeting spanning rows of glassed-in offices with the names and titles of the occupants.

"Nice views."

He nodded. "I agree, but occupying a space enclosed by glass has its advantages and disadvantages. There're times when I find myself staring out the window daydreaming." Giles nodded and greeted employees he rarely saw because he didn't spend much time in his office. His fingers tightened on Mya's waist. "My office is at the end of the hall."

"Where are your father's and brother's offices?"

"They're in what everyone refers to as the West Wing. Legal, accounting and cyber security are thought of as the heart of the company, while all of the other departments are its lifeblood."

"How many people do you employ?" Mya asked.

"The last count was thirty-eight. We have a number of real estate agents based in upstate New York, Massachusetts, Connecticut, New Jersey and as far south as D.C. They come into the office the second Friday in the month for a general meeting, while the board meets the first Monday of each month."

"Do they expect you to attend those meetings?"

"I just got special dispensation from my uncle Edward to participate using videoconferencing because of Lily. It's a perk all Wainwrights are afforded whenever there's a new baby."

"I suppose it pays to be a Wainwright around here."

Giles pulled her closer to his side. "You've got that right." He wanted to tell Mya that doors would open and Lily given full discretionary privilege if she was Lily Wainwright rather than Lily Lawson.

He opened the door and was met with a bright smile from Jocelyn sitting in an alcove outside his private office. "Hello, boss. Thanks for holding it down," Giles said teasingly."

Jocelyn's smile got even wider. "I had the world's best teacher."

Giles turned to Mya. "Mya, I'd like you to meet Jocelyn Lewis, the third woman in my with life whom I cannot live without. Jocelyn, Mya Lawson."

Jocelyn extended her hand and Mya took it. "It's a pleasure. Giles told me about you and your precious daughter." She pointed to the ruby on Mya's left hand. "Your ring is beautiful."

The skin around Mya's eyes crinkled in a smile. "Thank you." She patted Giles's shoulder. "And thank you for keeping my man sane. He says you're invaluable." Jocelyn lowered her eyes with the compliment.

Giles could've kissed Mya at that moment. He liked the comment about him being her man. "Are there any updates since our last email?"

"No. But I'm expecting a call from Kurt this afternoon about the Pederson deal. As soon as I hear anything, I'll update you."

"Thanks, Jocelyn. I'm going to see my father before we leave. You know how to reach me."

"She is very pretty," Mya said once they were far enough away so Jocelyn couldn't overhear them. Jocelyn's demeanor indicated she was older than Mya, but she felt envious of the woman's flawless complexion. Her chemically straightened hair, parted off-center, ended at her jawline, and there was a subtle hint of color on her full mouth while the only allowance she made for eye makeup was mascara.

"Jealous, sweets?" Giles teased.

"Should I be?"

"Never. Remember, I'm committed to you until Lily graduates college."

"What happens after that?"

Giles stopped, nearly causing Mya to lose her balance. He pulled her over into an area with a low table cradling a large fern growing in a painted glazed pot. "What do you mean by what happens after that?"

"Will we still be together?"

His brows lowered in a scowl. "What do you think?"

Mya stomped her foot. "Why are you answering my question with a question?"

"Because you're not making sense, Mya. What do I have to do or say to convince you that I'm just not in this for Lily? Even if you decide not to marry me I'll buy a house in Wickham Falls and come to see Lily everyday so she can grow up knowing that I'm her father."

Mya felt a fleeting panic grip her until she found it hard to breathe. She didn't want to lose Giles, because she needed him, needed him for more than a physical craving that grew stronger with each passing day. She needed him to love her and to restore her faith in men; after dating Malcolm, she still harbored a fear that she would become involved with another Jekyll and Hyde.

She found Giles even-tempered and soft-spoken, yet she sensed he could be unrelenting and uncompromising.

His expression changed, softening when he saw indecision in her eyes. "You've reminded me that you're not your sister, and I have to remind you again that I'm not your ex-boyfriend. What you see is what you get."

A trembling smile flitted across her lips. "You just read my mind."

"Let's hope you can't read mine because it would be rated triple X right about now." His eyes made love to her face before they moved lower over her chest. "Damn, woman. Do you know that you're sexy as hell?" he whispered in her ear.

Mya swatted at him. "Shame on you," she chastised, "talking dirty in the middle of a hallway where anyone can come by and hear you."

"There's a company policy about gossiping. One infraction and you're canned."

"That's a little severe."

"Spreading gossip is not only malicious but a form of bullying, and around here, that's grounds for an immediate dismissal. Come with me, baby. I want to introduce you to my brother."

Mya felt more in control when she followed Giles into an office next to his father's. The blond head popped up when the occupant realized he wasn't alone.

Patrick Wainwright stood up and winked at her.

"So you're the woman who has my brother stuttering every time he mentions your name." He rounded the desk. "Come and give me a hug."

The resemblance between Giles and Patrick was remarkable enough for them to be twins. The only difference was the color of their hair. Patrick was fair and gorgeous and Giles dark and dangerous. Mya found herself in Patrick's arms as he lowered his head and kissed her cheek.

"It's nice meeting you, Patrick."

He pulled back, holding her at arm's length. "I must admit my little brother has exquisite taste in women."

"Stop flirting with my woman or I'll tell your wife."

Patrick cut his eyes at Giles. "Nice try. You know my wife wouldn't believe anything negative you'd say about me." He lifted Mya's left hand. "Is that what I think it is?"

Mya smiled. "Yes. It's your mother's ring."

"Does this mean you and my brother are engaged? She shook her head. "No." Even though she was vacillating about whether she wanted to marry Giles, deep down inside it was something she wanted more than any else thing in the world. She had always grown up believing she would fall in love, marry and have children. She wanted a family of her own and to share all of the wonderful things her parents had given her.

The few times she and Sammie argued it was when Mya accused her of being selfish and ungrateful because their adoptive parents had given them what their biological parents hadn't been able to. She tried to make her sister see the flip side of their lives where they could've grown up living in squalor where hunger was commonplace instead of a rarity. They'd known kids they'd gone to school with who, if it hadn't been for free lunch or food stamps, they would have been malnourished.

Patrick kissed her on both cheeks. "Dad told me about Lily and I can't wait to meet her. I know my boys will happy to know there's another cousin they can play with. It's going to be a while before Jordan's little boy will be underfoot."

"You know Lily is the only princess among these young princes," Giles bragged.

"No shit," Patrick drawled. "We'll have to wait and see what Brandt and Ciara have."

"Ciara's pregnant?" Giles asked his brother.

"I don't know, but the last time I spoke to Brandt, he said they were going to get a jump on starting a family because he wants a football team."

Giles grunted. "There's no way Ciara's going to agree to having eleven kids."

"By the way, how many kids do you guys plan to have? I mean if you do decide to marry," Patrick blurted out.

Mya shared a look with Giles. They'd talked about marriage but not about whether they would have children together. Suddenly she felt as if she'd been put on the spot because she was wearing Amanda's ring. Patrick had assumed she and Giles would eventually marry, and wondered how many more Wainwrights would come to the same conclusion. "We'll probably have another two," she said after a noticeable pause.

"Why stop at three?" Patrick questioned. "Why not round it out and have four?"

Giles dropped an arm over Mya's shoulders. "Mya

and I would like to wait until Lily's walking and talking before we go back to changing diapers."

"I hear you, my brother." The phone on Patrick's desk rang. "I'm going to have to take that call. It's nice meeting you, Mya. If the family doesn't get to meet you and Lily before you guys go back to West Virginia, then it's Thanksgiving for certain."

Mya noticed Pat's office was empty when they retraced their steps to the elevator. "I hope folks don't assume we're engaged because I'm wearing your mother's ring," she said once they stepped into the car.

Giles crossed his arms over his chest. "People will always draw their own conclusions. Once we're officially engaged I'll buy you a ring."

She held out her hand. "What's wrong with this ring?"

"Nothing. I just believe a woman should have her own ring."

"If my birthstone was a ruby rather than a pearl, I would definitely consider a ruby."

"When's your birthday?"

"June 12."

"The month for weddings and graduations." He reached for her hand when the doors opened. If they married on her birthday, then he would have no excuse for forgetting their wedding anniversary. "Are you ready to go shopping now?"

Mya smiled. "Of course."

"Do you know where you want to shop?"

"Yes. I researched online and discovered a few shops on Madison Avenue that carry the labels I like."

"I hope I don't come to regret this," Giles mumbled under his breath.

"I heard that, sport."

"I wanted you to, sweets. Are you the type of woman that has to try on a dozen dresses and then decides to buy the first one she tried on?"

Mya rolled her eyes at him. "I'm not even going to dignify that with an answer."

Giles waved his hand and whistled sharply between his teeth to flag down a taxi. The driver came to a screeching stop at the curb. Giles opened the rear door and allowed Mya to enter, then slid onto the seat next to her. He gave the driver their destination and the driver took off as if he was racing in the Indy 500.

Mya huddled closer to Giles. "I hope we'll get there in one piece."

He buried his face in her hair. "New York City taxi drivers are notorious for weaving in and out of traffic."

She closed her eyes. "Let me know when we're there."

Mya found a boutique that carried the designs she favored. Several salesladies fussed over Giles as he sat in a comfortable chair in the seating area and was given green tea and sliced fruit while he watched a wall-mounted flat screen television.

It was too early for cruise wear, but the salesperson said they still had some items in stock from the beginning of the year. She wanted a few outfits for when she went to the Bahamas with Giles. Mya preferred shopping in specialty shops because of the individual service and there weren't endless racks of the same mass-produced dresses and blouses.

It took more than an hour for her to try on dresses, jackets, slacks, blouses, shorts and several swimsuits.

When the assistant helping asked if she wanted her boyfriend to see her in anything, Mya told her no, because she wanted to surprise him. She wasn't certain whether Thanksgiving and Christmas were semiformal events for the Wainwrights so she chose several dresses that she deemed appropriate. Mya thought about asking to see formal wear for the New Year's Eve fund-raiser, and then changed her mind. She decided to wait until they came back for Thanksgiving to shop for a dress. It would signal the beginning of holiday shopping and she knew she would be able to select something appropriate for the event.

"I suppose that's it," she said to the assistant who'd help her into and out of garments.

The woman smiled. "I'll take these up front while you get dressed."

When Mya emerged from the dressing room, she found Giles at the register as the cashier rang up her purchases. He pushed her hand away when she handed him her credit card. "Put *that* away," he ordered between clenched teeth. He took it from her fingers and slipped it into his shirt pocket when she hesitated. "I'll give it back later."

He turned back to the cashier, offering her a friendly smile. "Could you please have someone deliver these to my apartment?"

The clerk glanced at the card he'd given her. "Of course, Mr. Wainwright. Is it all right if we deliver it tomorrow because deliveries for today are already out on the van?"

"Of course." He plucked a business card off the counter and jotted his name and address on the back.

The woman glanced at the address. "It should arrive before noon."

"No problem. Let the driver know he can leave it with concierge." He signed the receipt and returned the card to a case in his jacket's breast pocket. "Let's go, sweets. I don't know about you but I'm hungry enough to eat half a cow." He whistled for a taxi that sped by without stopping. "I'm going to order something and have it delivered to the apartment. What do you feel like eating?"

Reaching into her hobo bag, Mya took out a pair of sunglasses to shade her eyes against the glaring autumn sun. "Half a cow," she said, deadpan.

He splayed his hand over her hips. "You could use a little more meat in this area."

"I have enough, thank you." She wrapped her arm around his waist under his suit jacket. "Thank you for paying for my clothes."

Giles frowned. "There's no need to thank me, Mya. Whenever we're together, I don't want you to go into your wallet for anything. And I repeat—*anything.*"

"Oh, that's how it's going to be?"

"No. That's how it is."

Mya decided it was futile to verbally spar with Giles. Most times it accomplished nothing so she mentally accepted his mandate that he would pay for whatever she needed when they were together. After all, it was his money and he could spend it however he wished.

Chapter Ten

Mya sat on the balcony outside Giles's bedroom staring out at water views while enjoying the most delicious chicken piccata with a side dish of broccoli in garlic and oil she had ever eaten. And throwing caution to the wind, she had accepted a glass of rosé to accompany the meal. She had shed her dress, jacket, nylons and booties in exchange for one of Giles's long-sleeved shirts.

She closed her eyes for several seconds and turned her face up to the warm sun. "This is wonderful." She opened her eyes to find him watching her. "How often do you sit out here and have your meals?"

His lids came down, concealing his innermost thoughts from her. "Not enough. Whenever I sit here, it is usually to clear my head." A faraway expression swept over his features. "This is what I call my therapy place. When I first bought this condo, I would sit out here for hours until nature forced me to get up. At that time I was in a very dark place."

She recalled him admitting to experiencing post-traumatic stress disorder. "What about now?" she asked in a quiet voice.

He blinked as if coming out of a trance. "I'm good. Very good." Giles pointed to her half-empty wineglass. "Do you want more wine?"

She placed her hand over the top of the glass. "Please no. I'm surprised I'm having it when I'd gone down for the count after two beers."

"I do happen to have a bed where you can sleep it off," he teased.

Mya glanced over at the king-size bed with a massive dark gray quilted headboard. "I just might take you up on your offer." She patted her belly over the shirt. "Right now I'm as full as a tick on a dog's back."

Throwing back his head, Giles laughed. "I'm going to have to get used to your regional expressions."

"Like, if the creek don't rise, or she was madder than a wet hen."

"Exactly."

"Once you spend some time in the Falls, you'll become familiar with all of the expressions. I…" Her words trailed off when Giles's cell phone chimed.

He picked it up and read the text message. "My sister decided not to come. She says she'll see you and Lily at Thanksgiving."

"Is something wrong?"

Giles shook his head. "I don't know. Half the time I wonder what she's going through with that clown. I hope and pray he's not abusing her because it won't go well for him. My father is a laid-back dude, but don't

mess with his little girl because he can more dangerous than Uncle Wyatt."

"Do you think she would put up with a man abusing her?"

"Skye is a throwback to a flower child. She believes
in peace and live-and-let-live. She feels guilty that she
was born into money when there're so many people that
are hungry and homeless. When I suggested she donate
her trust fund to charity, she said she's wary of chari-
ties because the money will usually pay for administrative salaries rather than for the earmarked need."

"Why doesn't she set up her own charity? That's
what Sawyer Middleton did when he donated almost
a million dollars to update the technology lab at the
school. Not only does he head the charity, but he's also
responsible for overseeing the project. If she's a guidance counselor, then she can set up a counseling center for kids with emotional issues. And if she's really
ambitious, she can add a tutoring component and hire
teachers looking to supplement their income to help
students needing extra help with their schoolwork. I'd
be willing to volunteer to help kids struggling with
English."

Giles leaned back in his chair and pressed a fist to
his mouth. "I think you've got something there. I'll
be certain to mention it to Skye. She'd fit right in living in Wickham Falls because she's so unpretentious."

"There you go," Mya drawled. She pushed off the
chair. "I'm going to accept your offer to take a nap before we go back to your folks' place."

"Leave the dishes. I'll put everything away."

She walked off the balcony and into the bedroom.
Pulling back the white silk comforter, she slipped

under a sheet and lightweight blanket. "Are you going to join me?" she asked Giles when he entered the room balancing plates along his forearm.

"Later."

Giles wanted to ask Mya if she had lost her mind inviting him to share the bed with her. Did she trust him that much not to try to make love to her? Then he had to remember she would be the first woman to sleep there, because every woman he'd slept with since returning to civilian life had been in a hotel. It was as if the condo was his sacred sanctuary and he didn't want to defile it by having sex with different women. And sex was what it had been. He had never allowed himself to feel anything other than hormones calling out to one another for a physical release.

Giles didn't need a therapist to tell him he would've continued to live his life by his leave: spending hours in his office, traveling to the Caribbean and waiting for women to call him, if it hadn't been for Mya and Lily. He had made it a practice never to call a woman but waited for them to call him.

He put away the food and stacked the dishwasher. Spending time with Mya had enhanced his domestic skills. She'd shown him how to load and operate the dishwasher, washing machine and dryer. The last bastion for him to scale was learning to cook. Although he had balked, Giles knew eventually he would have to make an attempt.

He returned to the bedroom, slipped off a pair of walking shorts, leaving on his boxer briefs, and got into bed with Mya. Her back was turned to him. "Are you still awake?"

"Yes. I'm not as sleepy as I am relaxed."

He kissed the nape of her neck. "Good." A pregnant silence ensued, and he felt her suddenly go stiff. "What's the matter, sweets?"

"I was just thinking about Sammie sleeping here with you."

"She never slept here with me." Mya turned to face him, and he told her about the suite at a Chelsea boutique hotel where he conducted his affairs. "I pay for the suite every month even if I didn't use it. Something wouldn't allow me to bring a woman here."

Mya rested a hand on his cheek. "Until now."

He smiled. "Yes. Until now." Giles pulled on a curl that escaped the pins in the chignon. "There are times when I need you to be patient with me if I become somewhat overbearing. I suppose it comes from giving orders and expecting them to be followed without question."

Her fingernail grazed an emerging beard. "Did you enjoy the military?"

"I did because it was strictly controlled, regimented, and I needed discipline at twenty-one." Giles met her large, slightly slanting, catlike gray-and-green eyes. "I'd grown up believing as a kid of privilege I could do whatever I wanted and the hell with everything else. I went to a private school where infractions at a public school would've resulted in a suspension or expulsion, but because our parents were doling out the big bucks for tuition or bestowing substantial endowments, we got away with things that would've been questionable by law enforcement. Like a lot of teenagers, we drank, smoked weed, had sex with girls willing to give it up, and a few kids ended up in rehab because they got hooked on crack or heroin.

"I was an above-average student and was accepted by several top universities but in the end, I chose MIT. I continued to drink and smoke weed, but I'd become discriminating when it came to sleeping around because I knew I wasn't ready to deal with an unplanned pregnancy. My senior year signaled a change when I stopped hanging out as much and stopped drinking and smoking altogether. I managed to graduate with honors and Wyatt, who was at the time WDG's de facto CEO, asked me to join the engineering department."

"What did you tell him?"

"'Ask me again in three months and I'll give you my answer.' I was burned-out and needed that time to recharge. That's when my mother decided that her youngest son needed a steady girlfriend."

"Is that when your mother tried to set you up with Miranda?"

Giles nodded.

"But you were so young to think about settling down with a wife."

"I know that and you know that, but people in particular social classes are always looking for their children to make a proper match, much like an arranged marriage in some cultures. Once I discovered the subterfuge, I enlisted in the branch of the military with the toughest basic training. I met the initial requirements for officer eligibility and worked and studied harder than I ever had in my life to graduate Officer Candidate School. It was when I was mentally, physically and morally at my best."

Mya cradled his face. "You've come a long way from

that weed-smoking, skirt-chasing and binge-drinking boy to a man Lily will grow up to be proud of."

"And I swear if I find some pimply faced, pothead cretin sniffing around my daughter, I'll snap his head off and roll it down the street like a bowling ball."

Mya's laugh was low, throaty. "Why do men always talk about hurting a boy if they come around their daughter?"

"That's because we know what we've done to some man's daughter."

"It's called karma and payback."

Resting an arm over her waist, Giles pulled Mya closer until her breasts were flattened against his chest. "Karma is a very nasty girl."

"That she is."

Those were the last words she mumbled before Giles registered her breathy snoring. He had done something with Mya he had never done with another human being and that was to bare his soul. His parents never knew of his drinking and drug use either because he'd become so adept at concealing his destructive behavior or they were in denial, unable to believe their so-called model son was less than perfect.

"I love you."

Giles knew Mya couldn't hear him, yet he felt compelled to say what lay in his heart. He loved everything about her: her loyalty to her sister, willingness to sacrifice her career to take care of her sister's child and her feistiness when she refused to back down when he challenged her.

He was aware of her reluctance to share her life and future with a stranger and he was willing to wait however long it would take to convince her he wanted her as his wife with or without Lily. Mya had accepted the responsibility of raising his child with or without him, while offering him an alternative to a lifestyle where he had become so self-absorbed that his only focus was doing what made him happy.

Wickham Falls would not top his list of places to live and retire; however, he found himself looking forward to living in the Louisiana low-country style house with a woman and child that had him planning for their futures.

Giles's breathing deepened, and after a while he joined Mya in the comforting embrace of Morpheus.

Mya held Lily to her chest as she paced back and forth on the sidewalk while she waited for Pat to retrieve his car from the indoor garage. A freezer chest with jars of baby food and bottles of milk and water, a carry-on with Lily's diapers and clothes, a portable crib and a car seat sat on the curb.

"You are becoming quite the traveler," she crooned. "First you visited the Bronx Zoo and now you're going to Boston." Lily cooed and patted Mya's face with her small chubby hands. "You have tons of cousins so I want you to be on your best behavior when they meet you. We can't have them thinking you have no home training." She went completely still when she detected the familiar scent of Giles's aftershave and the warmth from his body as he came up behind her. His moist breath feathered over her ear. "I was just giving your daughter a pep talk about behaving."

He laughed softly. "She's my daughter when she misbehaves and your daughter whenever she's a good girl?"

Mya smiled. "You said it and I didn't."

"Isn't that what you implied, Mama?"

"Not in the least, Daddy."

Giles rested a hand on Mya's shoulder and he leaned over to blow Lily an air kiss who pulled at her hand-knitted hat in an attempt to pull it off. He gently brushed her hand aside. "Don't, princess. Once you get into the car, I'll take your hat off."

Mya reached up and adjusted Lily's hat. "We're going to have a problem once winter arrives because she doesn't like wearing hats or socks."

"That's because she's a free spirit."

"You won't think she's that much of a free spirit when she comes home from college in bare feet, one side of her head shaved and a boyfriend with a braided beard trailing behind her. And the first words out of her mouth will be, 'But, Daddy, I love him!'"

"And Daddy will throw him in a Dumpster where he belongs."

Tilting her chin, Mya scrunched up her nose. "Why so violent?"

"I'm not going to let anyone mess over my baby girl. Here comes Dad."

A black Lexus SUV maneuvered up along the curb and came to a complete stop as the hatch opened. Mya continued to hold Lily as Giles stored everything in the cargo area and then placed the car seat on the second row of seats. He returned to take Lily from her arms.

Mya gave her a kiss and then turned and walked back into the house. She didn't know why but she felt as if she was losing her baby, even though she had a responsibility to let Lily know she had a large extended family. What Mya feared was that as Lily grew older, she might eventually lose her to the Wainwrights.

Amanda, carrying several bags, found her sitting on a chair in the entryway. She was dressed for traveling: cropped khakis, pullover sweatshirt, running shoes and a cap bearing a Yankees logo.

"We're going to take good care of your baby."

Rising to her feet, Mya flashed a smile she didn't feel. "I know you will."

"I'll call Giles to let him know we've arrived safely."

She hugged her future mother-in-law. "Safe travels, Mom."

"Thank you, darling."

Mya was standing in the same spot when Giles returned and closed the door.

"What's the matter, sweets?"

"Nothing."

Giles didn't believe Mya. She looked as if she was struggling not to cry. His fingers curved under her chin. "She'll be back tomorrow."

Mya nodded. "I suppose I'll have to get used to sharing her."

"Remember, you're sharing her with her family."

"I know that."

"If you know that, then why the long face?"

"I really don't want to share her, Giles. When Sammie put her in my arms and made me swear an oath to love and take care of her baby, I interpreted that to mean she wanted me and not you, Amanda or Pat to be responsible for her. Now this is the second time that I've allowed someone else to assume that responsibility, and if you think I'm being selfish, then just say it."

Giles searched her upturned face, his heart turning

over when her eyes filled. "You're not selfish, Mya. You're just being a mom. You've been with Lily every day of her life, and when you wake up, you look for her and it's the same at night when you get her ready for bed. But today is different because someone else will put her to bed and do all of the things for her you would normally do. Her grandparents taking her away for a day or two is preparing you for a time when Lily will leave for a much longer period of time. Maybe it will be sleepaway camp or an out-of-state college."

"I can't even think that far ahead."

"Neither can I, but we both know it's going to come. You've been rehearsing for your role as Mommy for eight months, while I just got the part as Daddy, so it's going to take us time before we really master our starring roles in this production based on parenting. Characters may come onto the stage for a brief moment before disappearing and others may become major supporting characters that remain on the stage until the final curtain comes down. We are the protagonists and my parents and the rest of the Wainwrights are the major supporting characters. They're not going to leave the stage, Mya. They're going to become a part of Lily's very existence because that's what Samantha wanted when she added the codicil. She wanted Lily to know who her biological father was and connect with his family because that's what she'd wanted for herself."

Mya rested her head on his shoulder. "Thanks for the pep talk. You're going to be an incredible father."

He buried his face in her curls. Giles wanted to tell Mya that he wanted to a good father and an incredible husband. "Now that we don't have to concern ourselves with a babysitter, I'd like to make good on my promise to take you out to dinner to celebrate the release of your latest book."

"Where are we going?"

"I have a few places in mind."

"Should I wear something nice?"

Pulling back, Giles smiled. "Yes." He still hadn't decided where he would take her but he wanted to make the night a special one.

"I bought an outfit yesterday that may be appropriate. But..."

"But what?"

"I need shoes and accessories."

Shaking his head, Giles rolled his eyes upward. "More shopping?"

"I don't need you to come with me."

"Do you know where you're going?"

She laughed softly. "I'm not going to get lost, Giles. I've downloaded a maps app on my cell and if I want to find a particular store, then I'll just Google it."

"I suppose you'll do okay in the big city."

"Just okay? Remember I lived in Chicago for nearly seven years."

Giles wanted to tell Mya that even though Chicago was a big city, it still wasn't New York City with its five boroughs and countless neighborhoods. "While you're shopping, I'm going to visit a cousin. I'm going to give you the keycard to my apartment and leave instructions with the doormen to let you into the building. Meanwhile, I'm going to call a few places to see if we can get a reservation for tonight."

"Maybe I'll stop and get a mani-pedi." She ran her fingers through her hair, frowning when she rubbed the curls between her thumb and forefinger. "And if I have time, I'll try to get my ends trimmed."

"I'll give you my charge card in case you run out of money."

"You gave me back my card and I have enough of an available balance to cover what I need to buy."

"I want you to take it anyway and buy whatever you want. In fact, keep it. I'll call the company and have them overnight me another one."

"You may come to regret that decision."

Giles winked at her. "I don't think so, sweets."

Mya returned his wink with one of her own. "Do I have a spending limit?"

"There is no spending limit."

Her expression changed, amusement crumbling like an accordion. "You're kidding?"

"No, I'm not." One of the many perks of having a Black Card was no spending limit. He knew it would take Mya time to adjust to the changes in her life once they were married. She would not have to concern herself with standing in line at airport terminals to take a commercial flight because a single phone call would give her direct access to a private jet. She would no longer stick to a budget when it came to managing household expenses, and if she wanted a new car, she wouldn't have to negotiate with the dealer for discounts on optional features.

"Okay."

His eyebrows lifted questioningly. "Just okay?"

"Yes. I can't think of anything else to say."

Threading their fingers together, Giles brought his hand to his mouth and brushed light kisses over her knuckles. "Have fun shopping."

Her smile began with a slight parting of her lips before moving up to her eyes, and Giles felt as if he was staring into a misty gray pond with delicately floating water lilies. "Thank you."

He kissed the back of her hand again. "There's no need to thank me because there isn't anything I wouldn't do to make you happy."

"I am happy, Giles. Happy that you're Lily's father and happy that you're in both of our lives."

She eased her hand from his loose grip, turned on her heel and headed for her bedroom. Inviting her to come to New York with him signaled a change in Mya. She appeared less tense, with the exception of agonizing over not having Lily with her 24/7.

When he'd introduced her to his friend in the sports bar, the word girlfriend had come out unbidden, and despite her wanting to wait until next spring to announce their engagement, he had begun to think of her as his bride-to-be. When she had asked him to court her, Giles knew the tradition of a man dating a woman for a specific period of time before proposing marriage had come from her traditional mother's Southern upbringing.

Giles regarded Mya as a small-town girl with big-city sensibilities. She could navigate a city with a population of millions, but it was her small town roots that surfaced when she preferred spending hours cooking to eating at a restaurant. She said grace before every meal, kept the tradition of making Sunday dinners the most important meal of the week, and whenever she sat at her computer, it was to pen her novels and not post messages to her friends on various social media groups.

Giles did not want to fool himself into believing that

relocating from New York to Wickham Falls would be without angst. He would miss going into his office, interacting with WDG employees and sitting in on meetings with department heads and the board of directors. He wouldn't be able to pick up the phone and make dinner plans with his mother or join Brandt or Jordan at baseball and basketball games. The only constant would be the flights to the Bahamas, and the upside to that was the probability of Mya and Lily accompanying him.

His life had become a series of highs and lows. He'd graduated college with a degree in engineering but within months, he'd turned his back on his family when he'd enlisted in the Marine Corps. He'd taken to military life like a duck to water when graduating as an officer and rising to the rank of captain. But after facing and cheating death twice, he wasn't ready to challenge it again when he resigned his commission and returned to life as a civilian, unaware it would become the darkest period of his young life. And in reconciling with his mother, facing his post-wartime demons and joining WDG, he'd become the phoenix rising from the ashes to soar and come into his own as the head of the company's international division.

Giles smiled as he exhaled an audible breath. His life was good and he predicted it would become even better once he, Mya and Lily became a legal family.

Chapter Eleven

Jordan Wainwright opened the door and pulled Giles into a rough embrace. "I'm glad you came over because right about now I need some serious male bonding."

Giles studied his cousin. The brilliant attorney looked different. His dark hair was close-cropped and instead of being clean-shaven, he now sported a short beard. Giles noticed there were dark circles under Jordan's large hazel eyes. He'd earned a reputation as a champion for those less fortunate, and many of the residents who recognized him on sight had dubbed him the Sheriff of Harlem.

"You now have your son to bond with."

Jordan blew out a breath. "I love my boy to death but all he does is cry, pee, eat and sleep. Then he wakes up only to repeat the cycle."

Giles smiled. "That's what babies do. And as a new

dad, you have to sleep when they sleep or you'll end up falling on your face."

Jordan led the way into the maisonette. He and his wife divided their time between their Manhattan duplex facing Central Park and a house in Westchester County. "Do you want anything to eat or drink?"

"Why? Did you cook?"

Jordan flashed a wide grin. "I'm learning. Zee told me if I'm going to hang around the house for six weeks, then I should learn to put a meal on the table."

"How's it going?"

"I made chicken with dumplings last night. She gave me an A, so if you want to sample leftovers, I'll heat up some for you."

"No, thanks. I'm good." Mya and his mother had prepared a buffet-type breakfast.

"Sit down and take a load off your feet," Jordan said as they walked into the living room. "Zee's upstairs feeding Max."

Giles sat on a butter-soft leather chair. He'd always liked Jordan's apartment because of its proximity to the park where he had an up-close-and-personal view of the changing seasons. However, for Giles it had one drawback: the noise of traffic along Fifth Avenue. His condo, high above street noise and the pollution from nonstop vehicles along the FDR Drive, was his sanctuary, a place where he decided who came and went.

Mya had been the first woman, other than his female relatives, he had invited in. And she was the only woman to share his bed

Jordan stretched out long legs and crossed his feet at the ankles. "Sleep has become a premium around here. By the way, do you sleep when your daughter sleeps?"

"Not really. Whenever Lily takes her afternoon nap, I usually hang out on the porch reading or relax in the family room watching television." Giles didn't tell Jordan it was a time Mya jealously guarded whenever she retreated to her office to write.

"What about at night?"

"I don't sleep over."

A slight frown creased Jordan's forehead. "I thought you and the baby's mother were getting closer."

"We are." Giles candidly told Jordan everything that had transpired since he left New York to move into the extended stay hotel so he could see Lily every day. "I've gotten her to agree to consider announcing our engagement sometime next year, but even that is tenuous. She wants us to date before we take what we have to another level."

Smiling, Jordan tented his fingers. "In other words, you're not sleeping together."

"We did share a bed but nothing happened. Our relationship is different from boy meets girl, boy likes girl, and then they fast-track their relationship from platonic to intimate. Right now, Mya and I are still in the platonic stage."

Jordan angled his head. "I'm going to ask you a question, and you don't have to answer it if you don't want. Are you in love with her?"

"Yes," Giles replied without hesitation. It was the easiest question he'd ever had to answer. "I've never been in love before so what I'm feeling for her has to be love. I say that because she's the first woman I've known whom I want to see every day. I like that she can be serious and teasing at the same time. I love her strength, intelligence and her devotion to Lily. And I admire the sacrifice she's made to give up her career to raise her niece."

Jordan chuckled under his breath. "She sounds quite remarkable."

"She is. And on top of that, she's gorgeous and sexy."

Jordan sobered. "When you called me, I thought you were going to bring your daughter so we could meet her."

"I would have if she wasn't on her way to Boston to meet her grandma's people."

"Are they flying up?"

"No. Mom and Dad decided to drive."

Jordan went completely still. "Your father took time away from the office to go on a road trip?" Giles nodded. "But he never takes off. Only when he's sick. Which my father says isn't often."

Giles had to agree with his cousin. Jordan's father, Edward, was now CEO, and there was an ongoing joke throughout the office that Pat was looking to replace Edward once he announced his retirement. Giles knew his father did not want to take over the reins as head of the company. He loved heading the legal department. Pat was single-focused, a workaholic, a perfectionist and a control freak. Patrick told him that their father tended to micromanage everyone and everything in the legal department, and that's why Giles knew he could never work for his father.

"Dad took one look at Lily and it was like he'd become a different man. And because he isn't a first-time grandfather, I'm willing to bet having a granddaughter is the reason for the change. I remember my mother mentioning that he took off for two weeks when she had Skye, compared to leaving the office to drop Mom off at the hospital once she went into labor with me and Patrick and then going back to the office. Once she came home with his sons, he hired a nanny to help her out because he claimed his work was piling up and he didn't want to fall behind."

"Are you saying my uncle has a soft spot for girls?"

"What else can it be?" Giles saw movement out of the side of his eye and stood up when he saw Aziza descending the staircase cradling her son in her arms. "Hey, beautiful."

"Don't talk the talk if you can't walk the walk, playa," she teased.

Giles winked at his cousin's wife. "My playa certification expired once I discovered I had a daughter."

"When Jordan told me you were dropping by, I thought you were bringing your daughter and her mother."

Aziza Fleming-Wainwright sat on the love seat next to her husband and then placed the infant in his arms. The new mother wore a white man-tailored shirt over a pair of black leggings and had styled her shoulder-length dark hair into a loose ponytail. When Jordan had introduced Aziza as his fiancée, Giles hadn't been able to resist staring at the tall, brown-skinned, slender woman with large, round dark eyes in a doll-like face with a hint of a dimpled chin. And when she'd smiled at him, he'd been completely enthralled with her.

Aziza's connection with the Wainwrights began years before she met Jordan. Their cousin Brandt had been and still was her client whenever she reviewed his NFL contracts and now his business projects. Jordan confided that he'd had to work hard to convince

Aziza to marry him because she had been burned by a disastrous first marriage.

"She's on her way to Boston because my mother wants to show her off to her relatives."

Jordan chuckled. "Aunt Mandy must be over the moon now that she has a granddaughter."

Giles nodded, smiling. "You're right about that." He told Jordan and Aziza they probably wouldn't get to meet Lily and Mya until Thanksgiving. "We'll be back again for Christmas and stay until after the New Year."

"You guys are welcome to spend a couple of nights with us," Aziza said.

"I'll definitely run it past Mya." Giles was certain Mya would probably want to hang out with Jordan and Aziza because they all were around the same age. "Who are the designated babysitters for New Year's Eve?" he asked Jordan.

"My sisters Chanel, Stephanie and Keisha have volunteered to monitor the childcare center."

A suite in the Wainwright family mansion had been transformed into a permanent nursery with cribs, youth and bunk beds. Another area had been set aside as a playroom rivaling those at some fast-food restaurants.

Soft grunting from Maxwell garnered everyone's attention. The infant had inherited his father's swarthy complexion and his mother's features. Sparse dark hair covered a perfectly rounded little head.

Jordan wrinkled his nose. "I think somebody needs to be changed."

Aziza reached for her son. "I'll do it."

Waiting until Aziza took the baby upstairs, Giles asked Jordan, "You don't change diapers?"

Jordan rubbed a hand over his bearded jaw. "Not if I don't have to." His hand stilled. "You change diapers?"

Giles nodded. "I've been certified as a Mister Mom. I've learned to diaper, feed and bathe Lily."

"There's no doubt you've earned your Daddy certification. I took off six weeks to help Zee around the house. We still use the cleaning service, but there's laundry and cooking. Now that I no longer have a live-in housekeeper I've learned to operate the washer and dryer and fold clothes. Instead of going to the supermarket, we now order online and have the groceries delivered." Shaking his head, Jordan blew out a breath. "I can't even begin to imagine what a single mother has to go through caring for her new baby and keeping her house in order and still remain sane. And those who make it look easy are definitely superwomen."

Giles knew exactly what Jordan was talking about. Before he'd stepped in to help Mya with Lily, she had done it all. "I hear you, cousin."

Crossing his arms over his chest, Jordan gave Giles a prolonged stare. "How are you adjusting to life in the country? Have you traded your luxury SUV for a pickup with a gun rack?"

"That's not funny, man. When I first got there, I was ready to cut and run, but now I can't wait to get back." He held up a hand. "Don't get me wrong, Jordan. I love New York but I think of Wickham Falls like finding an oasis in the desert. It's where I'm able to feel at peace with myself and everything around me."

"Maybe it has something to do with your new family."

"Maybe," he conceded. "Or maybe it goes beyond Mya and Lily. There are times when it's so quiet I can hear crickets in the daytime. Wickham Falls looks like a picture postcard with mountains, forests, waterfalls and white-water rapids. Once Lily's older, I'm going to teach her to swim in a lake rather than in a pool. I want to take her fly-fishing and white-water rafting. And because we live in a rural area, I'll also teach her to handle a rifle and a handgun. And of course whenever we come to New York I'll take her to most of the sporting events."

"So it looks as if you have your future all mapped out."

"Not really. Those are just some of the things on my wish list. I..." His words trailed off when his cell phone vibrated in the back pocket of his jeans. Rising slightly, he retrieved the phone and answered the call. It was a store calling to ask if his charge card was missing or stolen. "No, the card isn't stolen. I gave the card to Miss Lawson for her use. Thanks for calling." Giles ended the call. "Sorry about that. I gave Mya my charge card and a store clerk thought she'd stolen it."

"What you need to do is apply for one in her name."

"I've already done that." He'd called the credit card company earlier that morning and requested an additional card for an authorized user. Giles glanced at his watch. He stood up. "I have to head out now because I have a three o'clock appointment with my barber."

Jordan pushed to his feet. "I know you have your itinerary planned out in advance while you're here, so I guess we'll see you guys for Thanksgiving."

"You bet." Giles's parents were hosting Thanksgiving, while Jordan's parents had assumed the responsibility of planning Christmas. He hugged Jordan again before taking his leave. "Kiss Aziza and that beautiful boy for me. I'll see you guys next month."

Giles left the maisonette, walking east to Lexington Avenue where he hailed a cab to take him downtown. He'd called a former high school classmate who recently opened an intimate restaurant with a piano bar on a quiet block between First and Second Avenue and within walking distance of his Sixty-Second Street apartment. He knew Mya was in a funk because it was the first time since Lily came home from the hospital that she hadn't been there with and for her, and Giles hoped eating out and listening to music for several hours would help to lift her dark mood.

If Mya entertained doubts as to whether Giles would approve of her outfit, they vanished completely when she walked into the living room to find him waiting for her. He stared at her as if she was a stranger as he slowly rose to his feet. She held her hands out at her sides.

"I hope I'm not overdressed."

Giles blinked once. "Oh my... I... I don't," he stuttered, seemingly unable to get the words out. He cleared his throat. "You are beyond perfection."

She'd chosen to wear a sleeveless, high-necked, mid-calf, ruby-red, lace sheath dress with an attached black underslip. Black silk-covered, four-inch stilettos and an evening clutch completed her elegant look. A stylist had trimmed the ends of her curly hair just above her shoulders; each time she turned her head, the loose gold-streaked curls moved as if they'd taken on a life of their own.

He headed toward her, and Mya recognized lust

shimmering in the depths of his electric-blue eyes at the same time a shudder of awareness eddied through her. At that moment, she felt an intense physical awareness that was frightening and palpable.

Giles leaned into her. "You smell and look good enough to eat."

Mya was helpless to stop the swath of heat that began in her face before slowly moving to her chest and even lower. She knew it had been a long time since she'd made love with a man, yet she did not know if she wanted that man to be Lily's father. Not before she sorted out if what she was beginning to feel for him was love or simply a need that reminded her she was a woman who'd denied her femininity for far too long.

"I think we'd better leave now before we're late," she lied smoothly. Mya knew if they lingered, then she would beg Giles to strip her naked, take her into the bedroom and make love to her.

Giles picked up his jacket off a chair and slipped his arms into the sleeves, and then handed Mya her black cashmere shawl. He waited for her to wrap it around her shoulders before reaching for her hand and leading her out of the apartment and down the hall to the elevator.

She averted her eyes as he continued to stare at her during the ride to the lobby. It was the first time since meeting Giles that she wasn't as comfortable and confident with him, and she attributed her uneasiness to the realization that her pretense of keeping him at a distance was nothing more than a smoke screen for her true feelings: she was in love with Giles Wainwright.

Although she had stopped thinking of him as her sister's lover, Mya was still attempting to sort out if

Giles wanted her for herself and not just because she was Lily's mother. And whenever she thought about Sammie adding the codicil to the will, she wondered if her sister wanted her and Giles together because she probably knew how much family meant to him. Mya had witnessed for herself that the bond between the Wainwrights was strong and invincible. They'd embraced her as if she had given birth to Lily, and before Giles's sister postponed her travel plans, Skye had been ready to drop everything to fly across the country to meet her niece.

It was as if her life had come full circle: she had been adopted by a couple who had given her everything a child could want or need, and now years later, she had adopted a baby and she and Lily were now a part of a large family who would give her daughter everything she could want or need.

"What are you thinking about?" Giles asked, once the car stopped at the lobby.

"Lily."

"What about her?"

"How blessed she is to have a big family."

Giles tucked Mya's hand into the bend of his elbow as they exited the elevator car. "Her blessings came from Sammie sacrificing her life to give birth to a healthy baby, and the second from having you as her mother."

"You're saying that because you're biased."

"No, I'm not. Seeing you with Lily has allowed me to see women and mothers in particular in a whole new light.

"Even though my mother grew up with nannies and live-in help, she didn't want the same for her children because she claimed she saw her nanny more than her mother. I remember her and Dad arguing constantly about having a resident cook and live-in housekeeper. In the end, Mom compromised when she allowed for a cleaning service to come in twice a week to clean the townhouse. She claimed she felt uncomfortable with having strangers living in her home with her children."

"I agree with her," Mya said. "Our house isn't *that* big that I can't maintain it." Although the house where she'd grown up was larger than many of the homes in Wickham Falls, it wasn't ostentatious. When her father hired an architect to design the house, he'd planned on having at least four children. The plans included two full baths, a half bath, five bedrooms that included the master bedroom on the main level with easy access to the veranda.

Graham had insisted on woodburning fireplaces and window seats in every bedroom, and a fireplace in the living room. The architect had divided the downstairs space into three zones: the front for two formal rooms for entertaining and dining, to the rear was the family room and kitchen with an eating area off the outside porch, and the third was the main-floor master bedroom suite.

Then there was the flower garden because Graham knew how much his bride-to-be loved tending her rose garden. He'd hired a landscape architect to create a garden on the one-acre property with flowers, trees, ornamental grasses and aromatic herbs. Every Saturday morning after breakfast, Veronica could be found in her garden, weeding and pruning her collection of hybrid roses. Now a landscaping crew came every week beginning in the spring to mow the grass and maintain the garden until early November when the flower beds were covered to protect them from wildlife foraging for food during the winter months.

Giles smiled when Mya said *our house*. It was apparent she had begun to think of them sharing a future where they would eventually live under one roof. "Our house is perfect for a couple with at least two or three kids. I'd like Lily to have a brother or sister before she turns two."

She shot him a questioning glance. "Please don't tell me you're planning for the next baby even before Lily begins walking."

Giles nodded to the doorman as he escorted Mya across the marble floor to the street. "I'm going to turn thirty-seven in February, and I don't want to find myself out of breath running after a toddler when I'm forty-five."

"There are a lot of men who have kids in their forties and fifties."

"I'll be fifty-five when Lily's eighteen and by that time, I will have earned membership in the silver fox club. And I don't want my six-year-old embarrassed when his friends ask if I'm his grandfather."

"How many kids do you plan to have? And have you selected the woman who will agree to bear your children?"

Giles stopped in midstride, nearly causing Mya to trip and fall. He caught her, holding onto her arm to steady her. "Did you think I was thinking of someone other than you?

She blinked slowly, reminding him of an owl. "I don't know what to think, Giles. I can't understand why you continue to make plans for us without talking to me first."

Giles felt properly reprimanded. He knew Mya was right because he hadn't had to think of anyone else but himself until now. He was single-focused when it came to securing Lily's future and he figured Mya would just go along with whatever he proposed. Unknowingly he had become his father, micromanaging Mya's life and expecting her to agree with his decisions.

He cradled her face between his hands. "I'm sorry, sweets. I've spent so many years doing what I want that it's going to take some time for me include others in my decision-making."

Mya's eyes clung to his. "You can make all of the decisions you want when you're at your office, but at home you're going to have to discuss things with me before we can compromise on anything that impacts our future."

"Yes, boss."

She lowered her eyes. "I'm not your boss."

"You think not," Giles teased. He pressed a kiss on her fragrant curls. "Let's go before we lose our table."

They continued to the corner and waited for the light to change. "I'm sorry, Giles."

Giles registered raw emotion in Mya's apology. "What are you sorry about?"

"I didn't mean to bite your head off, but I don't want you to forget that we're not even engaged and meanwhile you're talking about having more children. I'd believed I would raise Lily as a single mother. That I could be mother and father, but now I know I was deluding myself when I recall my own childhood. As a child, I loved coming home from school to find my mother in the kitchen preparing the evening meal. But the highlight of the night was when my father arrived because he'd open the door and yell in a perfect Ricky Ricardo imitation, 'Honeys, I'm home.' I thought he was just greeting my mother but he kept calling for his honeys. After a while, I knew he wanted me and Sammie, too. Then all of us would have a family hug and Daddy would say how much he loved his girls. That hug said more than words. It meant we were a family and nothing or no one could break that bond. That's what I want for you, me and Lily."

"And that's what we'll have. A bond that will last all of our lives." An expression of triumph and satisfaction showed in Giles's eyes.

Chapter Twelve

Mya, holding onto Giles's hand, slowly made her way down a flight of stairs to Dewey's Hideaway, a below-street-level restaurant. She didn't know what to expect but it definitely wasn't the grotto-like eating establishment with the only illumination coming from a wood-burning fireplace, a backlit indoor waterfall, dimmed recessed lights and the candles on nearly two dozen tables positioned close together to maximize space. Most of the tables were filled with diners, as the soft sound of the pianist playing show tunes competed with conversations and the distinctive rattling of serving pieces and plates.

"How did you find this place?" she whispered to Giles when she saw the hostess coming in their direction.

"A friend owns it." Giles smiled at the young woman

with neatly braided hair. "I have a reservation for two. The name is Giles Wainwright."

Picking up two menus, she lowered her eyes, then stared up at him through eyelash extensions. "Please come this way."

Mya didn't miss the flirtatious glance the woman directed at Giles. She seated them at a table not far from where a gleaming black concert piano sat on a raised platform. The hostess removed the Reserved sign from the table and walked away with an exaggerated roll of generous hips.

"How often do you come here?" Mya asked, as she folded her shawl over the back of her chair.

"Not often enough," answered a deep baritone.

Her head popped up while Giles came to his feet. She stared at a tall black man with a black bandana covering his head, chef's jacket and black pinstriped pants with Dewey's Hideaway and D. Dewey, Executive Chef stitched on the tunic over his heart. Giles and Dewey thumped each other's back in greeting. Mya found herself smiling when the two men began talking at once.

"I didn't want to believe it when my sister told me G. Wainwright made a reservation for two."

Giles pumped Dewey's hand. "Who did you think it was?"

"Your brother Patrick. When he calls to make a reservation, he identifies himself as P. Wainwright. He and his wife eat here at least once a month. She likes our mac and cheese with truffle oil." He winked at Mya. "Aren't you going to introduce me to your beautiful lady?"

Cupping Mya's elbow, Giles helped her come to her

feet. "Darling, this is Darryl Dewey, proprietor, chef and all-around good guy. Dewey, Ms. Mya Lawson."

Mya extended her hand to the handsome man with a complexion reminiscent of whipped chocolate mousse. The skin around his dark eyes crinkled in a perpetual smile. "It's a pleasure meeting you, Dewey."

Dewey kissed the back of her hand. "No, Mya. It's my pleasure to meet you." His eyes lingered on her left hand. "I don't know if your fiancé told you, but we go way back as far as the first grade."

"No, he didn't, but I'm certain he's going to fill me in," she replied. It was apparent Dewey thought the ring was an engagement ring.

"You guys can order on or off menu." He pounded Giles's shoulder. "I have to get back to the kitchen because we're down one chef tonight. I have your number, so I'll be in touch."

Mya sat down again. "Please don't tell me you two spent more time in the principal's office than you did in the classroom?"

Giles shifted his chair until they were seated side by side. "Wrong, sweets. Although we were best friends, we were also very competitive when it came to grades. When we graduated, Dewey's GPA beat me by one-tenth of one percent. He enrolled in New York University as a business major and, after graduating, went into investment banking. Dewey said although he made tons of money he hated it because his real passion was cooking. One day, he walked away from his six-figure salary and applied to the Culinary Institute of America to become a chef. He bought this place two years ago and now he's living out his dream."

Mya placed her hand over Giles's. "Are you living out your dream?"

A mysterious smile tilted the corners of his mouth. "I am. Before I met you, my sole focus was on work, and the harder I worked, the more I was able to convince myself that I didn't need or want anyone to share my life." He pressed his forehead to hers. "Meeting you has proven me wrong. Not only do I want you but I also need you."

Mya closed her eyes, too stunned to cry. Men had told they needed her, but they were glibly spoken words they believed she wanted to hear. She felt his hand shake slightly under hers and in that instant she was aware of the power she wielded over Giles. That he'd shown her vulnerability for the first time.

"I need you, too." Her voice was barely a whisper. "I need you to love and protect me and our daughter. When you go away on business, I'll be counting down the days until you return. And I want every subsequent homecoming to be as special as the first one. I know you want more children, but I want to wait and give Lily time to experience being an only child. I also need to warn you that I can be stubborn when—"

"Enough, Mya," Giles admonished softly. "You don't have to try and convince me that you're not perfect because no one is."

"Not even you?" she teased.

"Above all, not me." Cradling her jaw, he brushed a kiss over her mouth. "And I'll try and make certain every homecoming is more special than the one before it. We'll talk about you, me and Lily when we get home."

She nodded. "Speaking of home, I'd like to suggest

you give up your hotels and move in with your *fiancée* and daughter so we can begin living as a family. I'll fix up one of the bedrooms for you."

Giles pulled back, his features deceptively composed. "Are you serious?"

A slight smile softened her lips. "Very serious. You no longer need your love shack and you can stop polluting the environment driving between your hotel and Wickham Falls."

"Consider it done." Giles shifted his chair to sit opposite her, while resisting the urge to pump his fist. It was obvious Mya was willing to consider sharing her life and future with him. He did not tell her that he hadn't renewed the Chelsea hotel suite reservation for the month of October. Once he discovered he'd become a father, he realized he couldn't continue to have sex with arbitrary women to slake his sexual frustration. It had become a wake-up call that not only had his life changed, but he had to change.

Some of the guys with whom he'd attended college had planned to marry their girlfriends and start a family. They found it odd that he never mentioned having a special woman or marriage. At the time, giving up his bachelor status had not been an option. He had not wanted to be responsible for anyone but himself. However, fate had a way of altering his well-ordered lifestyle when he unknowingly became a father. Even the best-laid plans were known to go awry.

The spell that Mya had unknowingly woven wrapped him in a cocoon of peace. The newfound joy was shattered when a waiter came to take their drink order.

It was as if any and every other woman Giles had

dated ceased to exist as he shared nearly ninety minutes of eating, talking and listening to live music. The four-course meal began with a toast to her latest novel and followed with a salad of bitter chicories paired with crisp lardoons, toasted pine nuts and crumbled feta tossed with red wine vinegar and extra-virgin olive oil; the salad was followed with an appetizer of baked clams and entrées of marinated grilled skirt steak and shrimp scampi with side dishes of macaroni and cheese and linguine with garlic and oil. Their waiter had suggested sparkling white peach sangria as a cocktail, which had become an excellent complement for the expertly prepared dishes.

"Are you under the influence?" Giles asked Mya after she'd drained her wineglass. He noticed she did not take a sip of the wine concoction until after she'd finished the first two courses.

She smiled and the flame from the flickering votive cast flattering shadows over her delicate features and highlighted her hazel eyes with a golden glow. "Surprisingly, no. Maybe it's because I ate first." She touched the napkin to the corners of her mouth. "I see why your sister-in-law orders the mac and cheese. It's insanely delicious."

Giles wanted to tell Mya that she was insanely beautiful in red. Her palomino-gold skin reminded him of liquid gold, and his mother had chosen wisely when she gave Mya the ruby and diamond ring. As a young boy, he would watch his mother go through the jewelry she had inherited from her grandmother and meticulously select what she wanted to wear for a luncheon with her friends or a formal event with her husband. He remembered his elderly grandmother telling him that while some women in her social circle collected wealthy husbands, she preferred priceless jewels. He wondered if Mya would continue the tradition of giving the ring to their granddaughter.

Giles shook his head. He did not want to think of Lily marrying and making him a grandfather. At least not for a long time. He wanted to watch her grow up from infant to toddler, to young girl and teenager and finally a woman. He wanted to be there to cheer her successes and comfort her during disappointments. An unconscious smile crinkled the skin around his eyes. And more important, he wanted to be the role model for the man she would eventually chose as her husband and partner for life.

"What are you smiling about?" Mya questioned.

"I was just thinking about Lily making us grandparents."

"Bite your tongue, Giles. She's still in diapers, meanwhile you have her having babies."

He sobered. "You know it's probably going to happen one of these days."

"I know, but there's still so much I want to do with her before she's a woman."

Reaching across the table, Giles held Mya's hand. "And you will." He winked at her. "Are you ready for coffee and dessert?

"I don't think so. I am stuffed. The next time we come back to New York, we have to eat here again. Tell your friend that he's a gastronomical genius."

Releasing her hand, Giles signaled the waiter for the check. "I'll definitely let Dewey know you give him an A." He settled the bill, leaving a generous gratuity, and escorted Mya out of the restaurant.

She moved closer to his side. "It's really getting cold. Wearing lace in late October without a coat isn't very bright."

He looped an arm around her waist, sharing his body's heat. "It's chilly because we're not far from the East River." Her dress reminded Giles of the song "The Lady in Red." Raising his right hand, he whistled for a passing taxi.

"I think I can make it back to your place before turning into an icicle."

Giles opened the rear door to the cab when it maneuvered up to the curb. "We're not going back to my place. I figured we'd spend the night at my parents' house. I don't want you staying there alone and I want us to be there when Mom and Dad bring Lily back. My father always gets up early and is usually on the road before sunrise."

He did not tell Mya that if they did spend the night in his condo, he did not trust himself not to try to make love to her. And more important, he did not have any condoms on hand and he didn't know if Mya was using birth control.

Mya huddled close to him in the back seat. "I called my editor and was told she's in Europe for a book fair."

Giles buried his face in her hair. "Maybe you'll get to see her when we spend the week here between Christmas and New Year's."

"I doubt that. Publishing usually goes on hiatus that week. I'll probably hook up with her sometime next spring."

Meeting her editor in person was not a priority for Mya. Having Giles live with her was. She'd told him that she wasn't raised to shack up with a man and now she was going against what she'd been taught once she invited Giles to move in with her and Lily. Living together would offer her a glimpse into the life she would share with a man who'd roared into her life like a tornado that had touched down to sweep up everything in its path. Her emotions were strewn everywhere and once the twister was gone, she was left craving his touch, his kiss and wanting to know how it would feel to have him inside her.

"Speaking of spring," Giles said after a pregnant silence, "I know I'm fast-forwarding almost two years, but do you want a spring or summer wedding?"

"I'd like a late-spring wedding. It can get quite hot and uncomfortable in the summer."

He went still, and then his head popped up as he met her eyes. "You want to get married in Wickham Falls?"

"Of course."

"Is there a venue large enough to accommodate our family and friends?"

Mya nodded. "We can hold the ceremony and reception in a hotel off the turnpike or interstate."

"Would it bother you if I hire a wedding planner?"

She gave him an incredulous look. "Of course not. Did you think I would object?"

"I don't know. You've ragged me enough about not checking with you when making decisions that affect both of us."

Mya lowered her eyes. "You would remind me of that."

"Only because I don't want you to think I'm trying to run your life. I'd like to hire Signature Brides. Even though they're based in New York, I'm certain they would like to add another Wainwright wedding to their long list of high-profile weddings. They were responsible for coordinating my cousin Jordan's wedding and now they're involved in planning Brandt's destination wedding."

"You can hire them. All I want to do is show up and enjoy our special day."

"Would you like to become a June bride?"

She smiled. "Yes."

Giles retrieved his cell phone from the breast pocket of his suit jacket and tapped the calendar icon. "Your birthday falls on a Sunday. Would you like to share your anniversary with your birthday?"

She buried her face against his neck. "Of course not. It will give me an excuse to celebrate not once, but twice."

"And I don't have an excuse that I forgot our anniversary."

Mya laughed softly. "Something tells me that you don't forget much."

"Not when it comes to you."

Mya stared through the glass of the French doors. She'd returned to Wickham Falls in time to join in the town's Halloween festivities, while counting down the days when she, Giles, and Lily would return to New York for Thanksgiving However, the weather had conspired against them.

The house would've been as quiet as a tomb if not for the tapping of frozen rain against the roof and windows. She was mesmerized by the ice coating the branches of trees and a carpet of white turning the landscape into a Christmas card winter scene.

But it was still four weeks from Christmas, and the plan to go to New York to share Thanksgiving with the Wainwrights had been cancelled because of ice and snow storms ravaging the East Coast from North Carolina to Maine. Flights were grounded and states of emergency had been declared by governors in all of the affected states.

She felt the warmth from Giles's body as he stood behind her. There were times when she marveled that he could enter a room so silently that she would look up and finding him standing there. He had moved into the house and into the master bedroom. To those who saw them together, they were a normal couple with a child, but behind closed doors, they shared everything but a bed.

His arms circled her waist as he pressed his chest to her back. "You're not writing today?"

Mya closed her eyes and rested the back of her head against his shoulder. "I don't feel like writing."

"Do you have writer's block?"

"No. I revised my schedule because I thought we were going to New York this weekend."

"I was looking forward to it, too. So it looks as if we'll have our own Thanksgiving here."

Turning in his embrace, Mya went on tiptoe and brushed a kiss over his parted lips. "I have so much to be grateful for. I never could've imagined being this contented. And you're responsible for that."

Giles affected a half smile. "Only because I love you."

"Not as much as I love you."

He eased back, staring at her as if she had spoken a foreign language. "What did you say?"

Mya knew she'd shocked him, because it was the first time she'd admitted what lay in her heart. "I love you, Giles Harrison Wainwright, and right now I want you to take me to bed so I can show you how much I love you."

Giles blinked once. "I don't have any condoms with me."

"You don't need condoms, darling. I'm on the pill."

Giles knew Mya could feel the runaway beating of his heart against her breasts. He and Mya had been living together for nearly a month, and during that time, he had been reluctant to seduce her in an attempt to get her to agree to sleep with him. He hadn't thought of himself as an overly patient man but somehow she'd proven him wrong when he decided to wait—wait as long as it would take for her to come to him of her own free will.

Bending slightly, he swept her up in his arms and, taking long, determined strides, headed for the rear of the house and the master bedroom. Giles placed her on the king-size bed and lay beside her. He threaded their fingers together. "Are you certain you're ready for this?"

"Yes."

Moving over her while sitting back on his heels, Giles's hands searched under the hem of her T-shirt, massaging the tight flesh over her ribs before moving up to cover her breasts. Her breathing deepened as he slowly and methodically undressed her, and then himself. There was enough light coming through the windows to make out her eyes. Her steady gaze bore into his as he lowered his head and kissed her mouth.

Giles wanted Mya because he found her sexy, sexier than any woman he had ever met. That he wanted her because he knew he couldn't have Lily without her. And that she unknowingly had cast a spell over him, bewitching him with her poise and beauty. She challenged as well as seduced him, and instinctively he knew he could grow old with her.

She extended her arms and he went into her embrace. Placing his hands under her thighs, he parted her knees with his and eased his erection inside her. She gasped once, and then moaned and writhed in an ancient rhythm that needed no prompting or tutoring.

The impact of their lovemaking matched and surpassed the ferocity of the ice storm lashing the countryside with its fury as Mya ascended to heights of passion she had never experienced before. She sought to possess Giles as he did the same with her. Her sighs from experiencing multiple orgasms had not faded completely when Giles reversed their positions. Burying her face against the column of his strong neck, she kissed him under his ear at the same time he growled deep in his throat and caught the tender flesh at the base of her throat between his teeth, leaving a visible imprint of his claim. She savored the lingering pulsing of his hardness inside her.

Her fist pounded the pillow beneath his head. "Why did you wait so long?"

Giles frowned up at her. "Wait for what?"

"To make love to me."

"I can't believe you'd say that," he drawled. "If you'd given me the slightest hint that you wanted me to make love to you, I would've had you on your back a long time ago."

She smiled. "I suppose that means we'll just have to make up for lost time."

Giles winked at her. "You've got that right, sweets."

Two weeks before they were scheduled to fly to New York for the Christmas week Mya felt as if her fairytale world had suddenly imploded.

The fear and uneasiness she'd managed to push to the recesses of her mind had suddenly had resurfaced. The man with whom she had fallen love, made love with every chance they got, and looked forward to sharing her daughter and their future with had deceived her.

She had just put Lily down for her nap and walked into her office only to overhear Giles on his cell. The door was slight ajar and she heard Giles talking to someone. Her step faltered when she heard him mention Lily's name. Her heart stopped, and then started up again when he said, "Her name should be listed as Lily Hope Lawson-Wainwright. Yes, Wainwright."

Mya didn't wait to hear anymore. She made her way down the staircase to the kitchen at the same time she tried to slow the runaway beating of her heart. What she'd suspected all along had become a reality. Giles had wined and dined, wooed, courted and proposed marriage because it was the only way he could claim his daughter. She glared at him when he walked into the kitchen.

"Hi, sweets. I thought you'd be upstairs writing."

"I don't feel very much like writing. Not after overhearing your conversation."

An expression of confusion settled into his hand-some features. "What are you talking about?"

"Lily Hope Lawson-Wainwright," she spat out. "How dare you go behind my back and —"

"Stop it, Mya!" Giles said, interrupting her. "It's not what you think."

"It's not what I think but what I overheard."

"Why were you eavesdropping?"

Mya's temper flared. "Eavesdropping? In my own home?"

He managed to appear contrite. "Maybe I used the wrong word."

"You're damn right you did." Giles moved closer at the same time she slipped off the stool, putting more distance between them. "Don't touch me." She held up a hand. "And please don't say anything because right about now I'm ready to lose it."

A muscle twitched in Giles's jaw. "Suit yourself." Turning on his heel he walked out of the kitchen.

Mya closed her eyes, willing the tears welling up behind her lids not to fall. How could she have been so blind? The silent voice had nagged at her not to trust Giles, but unfortunately she had ignored it when time and again Giles made decisions without first consulting her. She was not his employee or soldiers under command where he issued orders and expected them to be followed without question. It had been a while since she had to remind Giles that legally he had no claim on Lily, and it was apparent that he had forgotten that fact.

Chapter Thirteen

"I can't believe we had to wait until New Year's Eve to meet you for the first time."

Mya smiled at Giles's cousin's wife. She never would've guess that Aziza Fleming-Wainwright was the mother of a three-month-old. A black off-the-shoulder gown clung to the curves of her tall, slender body. "I don't know, but every time Giles and I plan to come to New York it's as if the weather conspires against us. First, an ice storm for Thanksgiving and then a blizzard with nearly two feet of snow for Christmas."

Temperatures in the northeast had gone from below freezing to mid-fifties and within days mounds of snow had begun to melt.

What she did not say was her relationship with Giles had gone from frosty to icy. They had become polite strangers living under the same roof, while Lily continued to thrive. She was walking, holding on to objects to keep her balance and had begun calling Giles 'Da-da.'

When Mya arrived earlier that afternoon she'd found the suites in the four-story, gray-stone mansion spanning a half block on Fifth Avenue filled with several generations of Wainwrights, and she hadn't seen Lily once Amanda discovered her granddaughter was in the nursery with the other young children.

There was a soft knock on the door before it opened and a young woman wearing a black backless gown with a full skirt swept into the room. Her chemically straightened hair was styled in a loose, curling ponytail. Mya knew without introductions that she was Ciara Dennison, Brandt's fiancée. During their first visit to New York Giles had pulled up several family photographs on his computer and given her an overview of each person. Mya had teased him about the two, very pretty African-American women definitely adding a bit of color to the overwhelming number of Wainwright blonds.

The diamond ring on Ciara's left hand caught the light when she held out her arms to Mya. "All of the guys were whispering about how beautiful you are, and I just had to come and see if they were blowing smoke," she said with a wide grin. "Girlfriend, you are stun-ning!" She drew out the word in two distinct syllables. "I'm Ciara."

Mya pressed her cheek to Ciara's. "And I'm Mya."

Aziza rested her hands at her waist. "I'm certain when people hear your names, they probably think of the two female singers."

Mya laughed. "I'd starve to death if I had to sing for a living."

Ciara patted her hair. "I'd probably do a little better than you because I can carry a tune."

Her clear brown eyes sparkled like newly minted pennies. "It looks as if we sister-girls are batting a thousand when it comes to scooping up these fine-ass Wainwright men."

"I second that," Aziza drawled.

Mya had to agree with the attorney and psychiatric nurse. Even if their men weren't Wainwrights, Jordan, Brandt and Giles were the heroes women fantasized about when reading romance novels. "Excuse me, but I have to see Giles about something." Lifting the skirt of her chocolate-brown strapless gown, she walked out of the suite.

Turning on her heel, she made her way down the wide carpeted hallway to the curving staircase leading to the great hall. The mansion was decorated for the season: live pine boughs lined the fireplace mantel as a fire blazed behind a decorative screen. Lighted electric candles were in every window, and the gaily decorated, twelve-foot Norwegian spruce towered under the brightly lit chandelier suspended from a twenty-foot ceiling. Many of the more fragile glass ornaments on the tree were purported to be at least two hundred years old.

The ball was in full swing with formally dressed men and women eating and drinking, and many couples were dancing to a live band. Someone tapped her shoulder, and she turned to find a young man with brilliant green eyes in a deeply tanned face smiling at her. "May I have this dance?"

Mya returned his smile. "Of course."

"Who are you here with, beautiful?" he whispered in her ear as he spun her around the marble floor.

"Giles Wainwright."

"It's just my luck you would be connected to the folks hosting this shindig."

The song ended and Mya barely had time to catch her breath when she found herself dancing with another man. This one held her too tight as he couldn't pull his eyes away from her chest. When she pleaded thirst, he led her to the bar and waited until she asked the bartender for a club soda with a twist of lime.

"How about another dance?"

"Dude, how about finding another woman to dance with." Mya turned to find Giles glaring at the man. "Move along," he added when her dance partner hesitated and then walked away.

"What's the matter with you?" Mya asked between clenched teeth. "Have you gone and lost your mind?"

The coldness in Giles's eyes reminded her of chipped ice. "You have the audacity to ask me what's wrong when I'm forced to watch you disrespect me when you flirt with every man salivating over your chest."

"Disrespect! You have a nerve to talk to me about—"

Giles's fingers curled around her upper arm. "Come with me. We don't need to air our problems in front of everyone."

"Problems? I don't have a problem. You're the one with the problem," she said as they wove their way through the throng and out of the ballroom. Mya followed Giles to an area near the elevator. She was too angry to acknowledge he looked magnificent in formalwear.

Holding onto her shoulders, Giles gave her a death-stare. "What the hell was that back there?"

"Nothing!" she spat out. "A couple of men asked me to dance and I saw nothing wrong with dancing with them. Now if you're going to go off every time I talk to a man, then I don't think we should be together."

"What do you mean that I'm the one with the problem?"

"You have a problem being truthful, and I'm angry with myself because I allowed you to lure me into a trap where you can get legal custody of Lily and change her name by marrying me."

"If you hadn't shut me out I would've told you about my conversation with my cousin. I was talking to Jordan about setting up a trust fund for our daughter."

Mya blinked as if coming out of a trance. "She doesn't need a trust fund because I've set aside monies for her future."

"Why is it always what you want for Lily, Mya? Can't you just this once include me in the equation. Lily's not only your daughter but *our* daughter. I know I can get ahead of myself when it comes to planning her future, but from now on I again promise to talk to you first before making *any* decision about her."

Mya smile mirrored relief. Giles wasn't planning to change Lily's name. "And I'll be certain to remind you of that in case you forget."

"You can do anything you want to me, but promise me you won't shut me out again."

"I'll think about it."

"While you're thinking about it I need to do this." Giles lowered his head and brushed a light kiss over her mouth.

She bit down on her lip as she fought back tears. "I'm sorry, babe, for not trusting you." She took a step and curved her arms around his inside his tuxedo jacket. "Can you forgive me?"

Giles cradled her chin, his eyes making love to her. "Of course I forgive you. But can you forgive me for going Neanderthal on you?"

"Yes. Now kiss me again before we go back."

Giles needed no further urging when he lifted Mya off her feet and kissed her with all the passion he could summon for the woman who'd stolen his heart. "What do you say we go upstairs and have a quickie before everyone rings in the New Year?"

Mya shook her head. "Don't you ever get enough?"

Throwing back his head, Giles laughed loudly. Before their heated confrontation, they had made love nearly every night. "As long as I can get it up, I'll never get enough."

Mya looped her arms through his. "Let's go back before folks come looking for us." Midnight would signal a new year where she could look forward to marrying a man who had promised to love and protect her and their daughter all the days of their lives.

Eighteen months had sped by quickly and Mya would celebrate not only her birthday but also her wedding day. She'd chosen Giles's sister Skye to be her maid of honor and Aziza and an obviously pregnant Ciara as her attendants. Giles had selected Jordan as his best man and Brandt and his brother Patrick as his groomsmen.

Mya had asked her future father-in-law to give her away and he appeared visibly overcome with emotion when he nodded mutely. The weather had cooperated. Bright sunshine and afternoon temperatures were perfect for a garden wedding.

She touched the diamond necklace Giles had given her for a wedding present following the rehearsal dinner.

The owners of Signature Brides had arrived two days ago to make certain the tent was scheduled to be up for the ceremony and coordinate with the hotel's banquet manager for the reception. There had been a steady stream of Wainwrights checking into the hotel over the past three days. Some of the men were talking about returning in the fall to go hunting. A few of her colleagues from college were also in attendance.

She adjusted the flowing skirt of her gown with white lace appliqued flowers and a trailing train. A pale pink belt with silk roses matched the underslip. In lieu of a veil, she had selected to wear pink and white rosebuds in the chignon on the nape of her neck.

The string quartet played a Mozart concerto as Skye, Aziza and Ciara processed down the white carpet with their partners. The entire assembly under the tent rose to their feet with the familiar strains of the "Wedding March."

Mya and Pat shared a smile before she turned her attention to the man waiting to make her his wife. She was smiling from ear to ear when he winked at her. She counted the steps that would take her to his side. He reached for her hand even before the judge asked, "Who gives this woman in marriage?"

"I do," Patrick announced loudly, as a ripple of laughter came from those under the tent.

Mya did not remember repeating her vows or when

Giles placed a wedding band on her finger. However, she did recall his long and passionate kiss when the judge told him he could kiss his wife.

When they turned to face those who'd come to witness their nuptials, Mya smiled at Lily who squirmed to escape Amanda's hold. "Daddy!" she screamed, extending her arms for Giles to take her.

Not only was she walking but she was also talking. A photographer and videographer captured the image of Giles holding his daughter while he curved an arm around his wife's waist. He had given Mya the necklace for a wedding gift, while she'd handed him a gaily wrapped box with a copy of Lily's birth certificate with a note that it was time to amend the certificate so their daughter could legally become Lily Hope Wainwright.

When Giles had walked into the lawyer's office what now seemed eons ago, he never knew how his life would change. It was better than he could have ever imagined. He'd claimed his baby and a woman whose love promised forever.

* * * * *

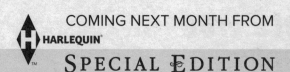

COMING NEXT MONTH FROM

HARLEQUIN®

SPECIAL EDITION

Available January 16, 2018

#2599 NO ORDINARY FORTUNE
The Fortunes of Texas: The Rulebreakers • by Judy Duarte
Carlo Mendoza always thought he had the market cornered on charm, until he met Schuyler Fortunado. She's a force of nature—and secretly a Fortune! And when Schuyler takes a job with Carlo at the Mendoza Winery, sparks fly!

#2600 A SOLDIER IN CONARD COUNTY
American Heroes • by Rachel Lee
After an injury places him on indefinite leave, Special Forces sergeant Gil York ends up in Conard County to escape his overbearing family. Miriam Baker, a gentle music teacher, senses Gil needs more than a place to stay and coaxes him out from behind his walls. But is he willing to face his past to make a future with Miriam?

#2601 AN ENGAGEMENT FOR TWO
Matchmaking Mamas • by Marie Ferrarella
The Matchmaking Mamas are at it again, this time for Mikki McKenna, a driven internist who has always shied away from commitment. But when Jeff Sabatino invites her to dine at his restaurant and sparks a chance at a relationship, she begins to wonder if this table for two might be worth the risk after all.

#2602 A BRIDE FOR LIAM BRAND
The Brands of Montana • by Joanna Sims
Kate King has settled into her role as rancher and mother, but with her daughter exploring her independence, she thinks she might want to give handsome Liam Brand a chance. But her ex and his daughter are both determined to cause trouble, and Kate and Liam will have to readjust their visions of the future to claim their own happily-ever-after.

#2603 THE SINGLE DAD'S FAMILY RECIPE
The McKinnels of Jewell Rock • by Rachael Johns
Single-dad chef Lachlan McKinnell is opening a restaurant at his family's whiskey distillery and struggling to find a suitable head hostess. Trying to recover from tragedy, Eliza Coleman thinks a move to Jewell Rock and a job at a brand-new restaurant could be the fresh start she's looking for. She never expected to fall for her boss, but it's beginning to look like they have all the ingredients for a perfect family!

#2604 THE MARINE'S SECRET DAUGHTER
Small-Town Sweethearts • by Carrie Nichols
When he returns to his hometown, marine Riley Cooper finds the girl he left behind living next door. But there's more between them than the heartbreak they gave each other—and five-year-old Fiona throws quite a wrench in their reunion. Will Riley choose the marines and a safe heart, or will he risk it all on the family he didn't even know he had?

HSECNM0118

Get 2 Free Books,

HARLEQUIN SPECIAL EDITION

<u>Plus</u> 2 Free Gifts—
just for trying the Reader Service!

SPECIAL EXCERPT FROM

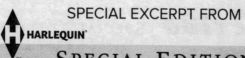 HARLEQUIN

SPECIAL EDITION

Special Forces sergeant Gil York ends up in Conard County to escape his overbearing family, only to run into Miriam Baker, a gentle music teacher who tries to coax him out from behind the walls he's constructed around his heart and soul.

Read on for a sneak preview of the second AMERICAN HEROES story, A SOLDIER IN CONARD COUNTY, by New York Times bestselling author Rachel Lee.

"Sorry," she said. "I just feel so helpless. Talk away. I'll keep my mouth shut."

"I don't want that." Then he caused her to catch her breath by sliding down the couch until he was right beside her. He slipped his arm around her shoulders, and despite her surprise, it seemed the most natural thing in the world to lean into him and finally let her head come to rest on his shoulder.

"Holding you is nice," he said quietly. "You quiet the rat race in my head. Does that sound awful?"

How could it? she wondered, when she'd been amazed at the way he had caused her to melt, as if everything else went away and she was in a warm, soft, safe space. If she could offer him any part of that, she would, gladly.

"If that sounds like I'm using you…"

"Man, don't you ever stop? Do you ever just go with the flow?" Turning and tilting her head a bit, she pressed a quick kiss on his lips.

"What the…" He sounded surprised.

"You're analyzing constantly," she told him. "This isn't a mission. Let it go. Let go. Just relax and hold me, and I hope you're enjoying it as much as I am."

Because she was. That wonderful melting filled her again, leaving her soft and very, very content. Maybe even happy.

"You are?" he murmured.

"I am. More than I've ever enjoyed a hug." God, had she ever been this blunt with a man before? But this guy was so bound up behind his walls and drawbridges, she wondered if she'd need a sledgehammer to get through.

But then she remembered Al and the distance she'd sensed in him during his visits. Not exactly alone, but alone among family. These guys had been deeply changed by their training and experience. Where did they find comfort now? Real comfort?

Her thoughts were slipping away in response to a growing anticipation and anxiety. She was close, so close to him, and his strength drew her like a bee to nectar. He even smelled good, still carrying the scents from the storm outside and his earlier shower, but beneath that the aroma of male.

Everything inside her became focused on one trembling hope, that he'd take this hug further, that he'd draw her closer and begin to explore her with his hands and mouth.

Don't miss
A SOLDIER IN CONARD COUNTY by Rachel Lee,
available February 2018 wherever
Harlequin® Special Edition books and ebooks are sold.

www.Harlequin.com

HSEEXP0118

Looking for more satisfying love stories
with community and family at their core?

Check out **Harlequin® Special Edition**
and **Harlequin® Western Romance** books!

New books available every month!

CONNECT WITH US AT:

Harlequin.com/Community

 Facebook.com/HarlequinBooks

 Twitter.com/HarlequinBooks

 Instagram.com/HarlequinBooks

 Pinterest.com/HarlequinBooks

ReaderService.com

**ROMANCE WHEN
YOU NEED IT**

HFGENRE2017R

THE WORLD IS BETTER WITH

Romance

Harlequin has everything from contemporary, passionate and heartwarming to suspenseful and inspirational stories.

Whatever your mood,
we have a romance just for you!

Connect with us to find your next great read, special offers and more.

f /HarlequinBooks

t @HarlequinBooks

www.HarlequinBlog.com

www.Harlequin.com/Newsletters

HARLEQUIN®

A *Romance* FOR EVERY MOOD™

www.Harlequin.com

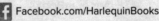

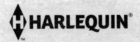